This month, in **CINDERELLA'S TYCOON**
by Caroline Cross, meet Sterling Churchill—CEO
of Churchill Enterprises. Nothing seems too big a
challenge for steely Sterling, until he finds himself
marrying Susan Wilkins—a plain-Jane librarian
who wants only to have her baby in peace in this
modern-day Cinderella love story!

**SILHOUETTE DESIRE
IS PROUD TO PRESENT THE**

Five wealthy Texas bachelors—all members
of the state's most exclusive club—set out on a
mission to rescue a princess…and find true love.

* * *

And don't miss **BILLIONAIRE BRIDEGROOM**
by Peggy Moreland, next month's installment
of the *Texas Cattleman's Club*, available in
Silhouette Desire!

Dear Reader,

Welcome to Silhouette Desire—where you're guaranteed powerful, passionate and provocative love stories that feature rugged heroes and spirited heroines who experience the full emotional intensity of falling in love!

Wonderful and ever-popular Annette Broadrick brings us September's MAN OF THE MONTH with *Lean, Mean & Lonesome*. Watch as a tough loner returns home to face the woman he walked away from but never forgot.

Our exciting continuity series TEXAS CATTLEMAN'S CLUB continues with *Cinderella's Tycoon* by Caroline Cross. Charismatic CEO Sterling Churchill marries a shy librarian pregnant with his sperm-bank baby—and finds love.

Proposition: Marriage is what rising star Eileen Wilks offers when the girl-next-door comes alive in the arms of an alpha hero. Beloved romance author Fayrene Preston makes her Desire debut with *The Barons of Texas: Tess,* featuring a beautiful heiress who falls in love with a sexy stranger. The popular theme BACHELORS & BABIES returns to Desire with Metsy Hingle's *Dad in Demand*. And Barbara McCauley's miniseries SECRETS! continues with the dramatic story of a mysterious millionaire in *Killian's Passion*.

So make a commitment to sensual love—treat yourself to all six September love stories from Silhouette Desire!

Enjoy!

Joan Marlow Golan
Senior Editor, Silhouette Desire

Please address questions and book requests to:
Silhouette Reader Service
U.S.: 3010 Walden Ave., P.O. Box 1325, Buffalo, NY 14269
Canadian: P.O. Box 609, Fort Erie, Ont. L2A 5X3

CINDERELLA'S TYCOON
CAROLINE CROSS

SILHOUETTE *Desire*®
Published by Silhouette Books
America's Publisher of Contemporary Romance

To the other Texas Cattleman's Club ladies:
Dixie Browning, Peggy Moreland, Metsy Hingle and
Cindy Gerard, four exceptional writers whose considerable
talents are matched only by their generous hearts.

Special thanks and acknowledgment are given to
Caroline Cross for her contribution to the
Texas Cattleman's Club miniseries.

 SILHOUETTE BOOKS

ISBN 0-373-76238-0

CINDERELLA'S TYCOON

Copyright © 1999 by Harlequin Books S.A.

Visit us at www.romance.net

Printed in U.S.A.

Books by Caroline Cross

Silhouette Desire

Dangerous #810
Rafferty's Angel #851
Truth or Dare #910
Operation Mommy #939
Gavin's Child #1013
The Baby Blizzard #1079
The Notorious Groom #1143
The Paternity Factor #1173
Cinderella's Tycoon #1238

CAROLINE CROSS

always loved to read, but it wasn't until she discovered romance that she felt compelled to write, fascinated by the chance to explore the positive power of love in people's lives. She grew up in Yakima, Washington, the "Apple Capital of the World," attended the University of Puget Sound and now lives outside Seattle, where she works (or tries to) at home despite the chaos created by two telephone-addicted teenage daughters and a husband with a fondness for home-improvement projects. An award-winning author who's been called "one of the best" writers of romance today by *Romantic Times Magazine,* Caroline believes in writing from the heart—and having a good brainstorming partner. She loves hearing from readers and can be reached at P.O. Box 47375, Seattle, Washington, 98146.

"What's Happening in Royal?"

NEWS FLASH, September 1999—Royal, Texas, is reeling from the news that illustrious business tycoon Mr. Sterling Churchill, CEO of Churchill Enterprises, has recently married Miss Susan Wilkins, librarian of the Royal Public Library, in a private ceremony at the city courthouse. *Obviously,* this was a whirlwind courtship!

Miss Wilkins *was* seen a number of times entering the Buddy Clinic—local lingo for the Buddy Williams Clinic for Reproductive Technology. Could it be a *baby* is the reason for the Churchills' surprise nuptials?

And just who *is* that regal blonde suddenly spotted waitressing at the Royal Diner? Do our Texas Cattleman's Club members have anything to do with her mysterious appearance from no one knows where? Our sources will tell you soon....

One

The telephone was ringing.

Head down, arms braced against the slick white shower tile, Sterling Churchill tensed at the shrill sound, the muscles in his back tightening reflexively beneath the pounding spray.

Why the hell doesn't Maxine get that? he wondered irritably a second before he remembered he was alone in the house. His return from Obersbourg earlier than planned had sent his housekeeper rushing off to the grocery store, muttering crossly under her breath about a certain person's lack of consideration.

Sterling snorted. After ten years in his employ, Max damn well ought to know he would have called if it had been feasible. As it was, he was just glad to be home, in one piece, the mission successfully completed. To the relief of everyone involved, Princess Anna and young William were now here safely in Royal, Texas.

He yawned. While the first part of the rescue had mostly involved a lot of time-consuming research and planning, once they'd put their plan into motion, things had happened fast. As a consequence, for the past week he'd operated on too little sleep and too much adrenaline, and it was finally taking its toll. As he'd unsuccessfully tried to tell Maxine when he'd gotten in that morning, he didn't care about food. All he wanted was a long hot shower and sleep.

Not that he was complaining. Lately his life had seemed increasingly empty, and he'd welcomed the break in his routine. He wasn't sure what it said about his character, but he'd relished the challenge of getting the princess out of Obersbourg, the small, elite country in Europe that was her homeland. And he had to admit that, despite the potential danger, he'd also enjoyed the adrenaline rush of eluding the Palace Guard as their small group—he, Greg Hunt and Forrest Cunningham, the princess and her little boy—made their way to the small, private airfield where their plane had been waiting.

Of course, the point was they *had* gotten away, he acknowledged with a grim smile. And it was a damn good thing. He didn't have a doubt that their involvement would have sparked an international incident had they been intercepted. Or that Prince Ivan of Asterland—the man determined to marry Princess Anna—would have pressed to see them jailed and prosecuted. It was just too bad for Ivan that they'd succeeded...

The phone continued to ring. Five, six, seven times—

Abruptly out of patience, Sterling straightened, turned off the water and shoved open the door. His feet barely touched the thick white throw rug as he launched himself across the marble floor. Snatching a burgundy bath sheet off the heated rack, he wrapped it around his waist and stormed into his oversize bedroom, stopping before the inlaid table next to the bed. He snatched up the receiver. *"What?"*

Dead silence was his answer. Thoroughly disgusted, he began to hang up, only to hesitate as a voice suddenly squawked, "Hello? Mr. Churchill?"

He brought the receiver back to his ear. "That's right. Who's this?"

"It's Mike Tarlick. Margaret's son?"

Some of his tension drained away. Margaret Tarlick had worked as a secretary in Sterling's main office at Churchill Enterprises until a car accident had left her seriously injured two years earlier. Tempering his voice, he said a trace more cordially, "Of course. Hey, Mike. How's your mother?"

"She's doing fine. She loves the new job, and it sounds as if she's even going to get a promotion."

Sterling stifled a yawn and glanced longingly at the vast expanse of his king-size bed. "That's great."

"We really can't thank you enough. If you hadn't continued to pay her salary and kept up her insurance and found her this new position—"

"It was no big deal," Sterling said uncomfortably. If there was one thing he hated, it was being thanked for doing the right thing. "Your mama's a real nice lady and a real hard worker. I just gave her a little head start. What can I do for you?"

"Actually it's what I can do for you, Mr. Churchill. I'm working as a tech at the Buddy Clinic these days, and I overheard something I think you ought to know."

Sterling scowled, his mood instantly deteriorating. The Buddy Clinic was local lingo for the Buddy Williams' Clinic for Reproductive Technology. Ever since

Sterling's marriage had gone bust, he'd done his level best to put the fertility clinic's existence out of his mind, associating it as he did with his most bitter personal failure.

"You understand, I could lose my job if Mrs. Richey ever finds out I called you," Mike went on, his voice growing anxious as he mentioned the clinic's director. "But I just thought…after what you did for Mom…this is something you have a right to know."

Sterling seriously doubted there was anything Margaret's son could tell him that he didn't already know. He and Teresa had undergone every test known to mankind, and the clinic still had been unable to come up with a reason why they couldn't conceive. Nevertheless… "You've got my word that I won't tell anyone I talked to you." Despite his level tone, he had a hard time stifling his impatience. After the past few weeks, he'd had all the intrigue he could handle.

"Good." Mike's relief was audible. "Because the thing is, I'm breaking all the rules of confidentiality…"

"Just tell me," Sterling said tiredly.

Mike took a deep breath. "Okay. I overheard two of the nurses talking. It seems there was a mix-up. A patient came in to be artificially inseminated and somehow the lab misread the code on the storage vial. The donor specimen that was used was…yours."

"What?" Sterling's head snapped up, his exhaustion suddenly forgotten.

"I don't know what happened, Mr. Churchill, honest. Everyone here is always so careful. Normally everything is checked and double-checked, but that day the regular lab manager was out sick and they had some temporary help filling in and—" he took a deep breath "—I wouldn't have bothered you, except that I pulled the chart and the test came back positive and I thought you ought to know.''

Sterling forced himself to concentrate as he tried to sort through the avalanche of information. Finally he said carefully, ''What test came back positive?''

''The pregnancy test,'' the young man said matter-of-factly.

For a second Sterling couldn't seem to breathe. ''The woman is *pregnant?*''

''Yeah. That's why I thought you ought to know. I mean, I'm sure Mrs. Richey intends to tell you, but first she'll want to meet with the lawyers and—''

''Mike?'' Damn. Dammit all to hell. Some stranger was going to have *his* baby? And he wasn't even supposed to know? Sterling took a deep breath, deliberately loosened the death grip he had on the phone and tried to sound calm. ''What's the pregnant woman's name, Mike?''

''Oh, I don't think…that is, I'm sure Mrs. Richey will want to be the one to tell you…''

Sterling squeezed his eyes shut. ''Please. I'd consider it a personal favor.''

There was another silence, the longest so far, and then Mike Tarlick said with obvious reluctance, ''I really shouldn't do this, but I guess…I mean, I suppose you have the right to know. It's Wilkins. Susan Wilkins.''

The name seemed vaguely familiar. Sterling struggled to put a face with it. For a moment nothing surfaced, and then it came to him. Susan Wilkins was that nondescript little redhead who worked at the library, the one who was a friend of Callie Langley's.

''Mr. Churchill? Are you there?''

''Yeah. Yeah, of course I am. I appreciate the call, Mike. I won't forget it. Thanks.''

"You're wel—"

Sterling dropped the receiver into the cradle, uncaring that he'd cut the young man off. Ripping the towel free of his waist, he strode toward the huge walk-in closet, his mind whirling.

Like it or not, sleep would have to wait. Not only did he have a call to make at the fertility clinic, but—more important—he had urgent business with a certain red-headed librarian.

Susan Wilkins strolled slowly along the sidewalk.

Stopping briefly before Cachet, the most exclusive of the many chic boutiques that lined Royal's Main Street, she took a moment to admire a sleek, pricey lilac-colored sheath on display in the window.

It was going on six o'clock. And despite a sluggish breeze that halfheartedly rattled the leaves on the big oak tree that stood sentinel down the street by Claire's, the town's best French restaurant, it was hot. The heat seemed to rise right off the concrete, burning through the soles of her worn leather flats and causing a trickle of perspiration to roll down her back. She could hardly wait to get home, take off her shoes, strip off her panty hose and exchange her work clothes for a pair of loose shorts and a T-shirt.

Yet she didn't hurry. And not because of the heat or her aching feet, which were courtesy of the two hours of overtime she'd put in at the Royal Public Library. Nor even because of the bone-deep exhaustion that seemed to weigh at her like an invisible anchor. And certainly not because of the dress. As pretty as it was, she had far more important things to spend her hard-earned money on.

Instead she stayed where she was a little longer simply

to savor the day. She admired the dress and basked in the brightness of the vast blue sky overhead. She drank in the sounds of the people coming and going around her and inhaled the faint scent of freshly cut grass coming from Royalty Park a few blocks away.

When she finally did resume walking, she couldn't help smiling a little at her uncharacteristic dreaminess. Or reflecting that lately she seemed to be floating on a secret sea of happiness. She'd felt this way for the past three weeks, ever since her pregnancy test had turned out to be positive. Finally, finally, her dream was coming true. She was going to have a baby.

She didn't kid herself that it was going to be easy. Money would be tight, and although the library allowed for an adequate maternity leave, she already dreaded the thought of leaving her child when the time came to go back to work. Still, it would be all right. Money wasn't everything, and she was rich in what mattered most: She had an abundance of love to share.

Besides, it wasn't as if this was a decision she'd come to lightly. She'd been considering it for years. And, as she'd told Mrs. Richey at the clinic, not only wasn't there a man in her life, but at twenty-eight, she wasn't getting any younger. Now that she'd finally been promoted to assistant head librarian, paid off the last of her college loans and managed to put aside a modest nest egg, the timing seemed right.

Thinking of Mrs. Richey made her remember that she'd forgotten to return the woman's phone call. It had come right at closing, when she'd been busy checking out last-minute patrons, and had simply gone right out of her head. She couldn't contain a smile. So far, a tendency toward forgetfulness and this constant exhaustion seemed to be the chief symptoms of her condition. Telling herself it could be worse—at least she didn't have morning sickness—she made a note to call the clinic director first thing in the morning.

Catching sight of her tiny rental house, she finally picked up her pace, only to falter as she caught sight of the man planted on her small front stoop.

Her stomach did a flip-flop. It was Sterling Churchill. Although she didn't know him personally—she didn't exactly move in the same social circles as powerful, self-made millionaires and men like him didn't patronize the public library—she knew who he was. How could she not? Not only was he a civic leader and a member of the prestigious Texas Cattleman's Club, like her friend Callie's new husband, Hank, but in a town the size of Royal, he was hard to overlook. She knew that he was in his mid-thirties, that as the CEO of Churchill Enterprises he had holdings in everything from cattle futures to oil wells, that he'd been married and was now divorced.

She also knew that he was big, dark and…compelling.

A wave of heat that had nothing to do with the weather rolled through her. She recalled the questionnaire she'd been required to fill out for the clinic, listing the qualities she wanted in her baby's father. The personality part had been the most important, of course. On it she'd stated that she wanted somebody kind, gentle and honorable, like her own father.

But there'd also been a section for physical attributes. She shifted uncomfortably on the hot pavement as she acknowledged that when she'd requested someone tall, lean and imposing, with dark hair, light eyes, chiseled features and a graceful way of moving, she might have been describing Sterling.

Yet there was no way he could know about that.

Could he? No, of course not. Nobody but the people at the clinic even knew she was expecting. And though she'd told Callie what she'd done, she trusted her friend to have kept her secret.

So what could he possibly want?

Before she had time to venture a guess he turned and caught sight of her. His gaze flicked over her, and something in his expression made her self-conscious. She glanced down at her mauve jumper, acknowledging that perhaps the calf-length hem and voluminous skirt weren't the most fashionable, and that the color might not have been the wisest choice for someone with her pale skin and auburn hair. And it probably didn't help that the hair in question was escaping its careful coil. Raising a hand, she wasn't surprised to find that the slippery mass was listing sharply to one side, while wisps snaked down her neck and tickled her temples and ears.

Still, that was hardly a reason for her visitor's jaw to suddenly bunch the way it did. Nor did it explain the decidedly cool note coloring his Texas drawl—so much more melodic than her own Northern diction—as he said gruffly, "Ms. Wilkins?"

As so often happened, shyness stole her tongue. Embarrassed, she ducked her head, and tried desperately to relax. After all, in roughly seven months she was going to be somebody's mother. How could she hope to take care of a child, if she couldn't handle a simple conversation?

Swallowing, she lifted her chin. "Hello, Mr. Churchill. May I help you?" *Oh, brilliant, Susan. You sound like the order taker at a fast-food restaurant.*

"We need to talk."

"We do?"

He gave her a don't-waste-my-time look. "We do."

Biting her lip, she crossed the sun-burned lawn and stopped before the single step to look up at him. Casually dressed in boots, jeans, a navy polo shirt and the Stetson that Susan sometimes thought was required dress for every man in Texas, he had an innate elegance that made her more aware than ever of her own woeful state. Clearing her throat, she said, "Is this about Callie and Hank? Are they okay?" ·

He stared at her blankly, then gave an impatient shrug. "As far as I know. Last I heard, they were still on their honeymoon."

"Thank goodness." She gave a sigh of relief and tried to explain the reason for her question. "I just thought, since we both know them, that you must be here because something had happened."

"It has. But not to them." He motioned toward the door with an abrupt jerk of his head. "Why don't we go inside?"

It was more an order than a request. Yet staring up into his cool gray eyes, she couldn't find the nerve to refuse. "All right." Glad for an excuse to look away, she fumbled in her purse for her house key.

She stepped up onto the stoop, sidled past him and unlocked her door. He was so close she could smell him, and the unfamiliar combination of aftershave, freshly laundered clothes and something else that was uniquely male made her hand tremble on the doorknob.

She walked gratefully into her dim little living room. It felt reassuringly familiar, not to mention refreshingly cool after the outside heat. Setting her purse on the small table next to the couch, she turned to face her guest, taking a surprised step back as she found he was standing right behind her, hat in hand. She sent him a tremulous smile. "Can I—can I get you something to drink?"

He didn't smile back. "No."

Suddenly desperate for a glass of water—her throat was so dry it was hard to swallow, and she really could use a moment to herself—she backed toward the kitchen. "I hope you don't mind if I get something for myself—"

"I understand you're not married," he said abruptly.

"What?"

"Do you have a boyfriend? Someone you care about?"

She stopped in her tracks and gawked at him. "I hardly think that's your concern," she said faintly.

"It is if you're having a baby. Are you?" He spoke as if he had every right to ask such a question.

"Mr. Churchill. Really!"

He took a step toward her. "Are you?"

Although she cautiously took a step back, his very intensity compelled her to answer. "Yes. Yes, I am. But how did you...that is where did you..." How could he possibly know? After all, Mrs. Richey had assured her of the clinic's strict rules of confidentiality, unless—oh! The phone call! That must be it. There must have been some sort of security breach and—

"It's mine."

She stared at him, certain she hadn't heard right. "What?"

"The baby. It's mine," he said flatly.

For half a second the room seemed to constrict, and then her common sense kicked in. She shook her head. "No. It most certainly is not. You—you—you're—" *Crazy.*

Of course! She felt overwhelming relief, followed by

a rush of compassion and a smidgen of regret as the harmless romantic fantasy she'd woven about him completely unraveled. Nevertheless, his being "confused" was the only rational explanation. Drawing a deep breath to steady herself, she said gently but firmly, "You're mistaken, Mr. Churchill. I don't know where you got this idea, but I assure you you're wrong."

"You're not pregnant?"

"Well, yes, I am, but—"

"Then it's mine."

"No," she said more sharply than she intended. "I mean—how could it be? I've never... And you and I most certainly have never..." Out of the blue, her imagination served up a brief but steamy vision of the two of them creating a baby the old-fashioned way. Mortified, she felt a betraying flush of heat rise in her cheeks. "That is, we've never even spoken before today," she said hastily.

"There was a mix-up at the clinic. My semen was used in your procedure."

She shook her head. "No—"

"Yes," he contradicted, his voice suddenly harsh. "How the hell do you think I know about this? About you?"

His vehemence silenced her. The truth was there, not only in what he said but in his grim face. "Oh, dear. Oh, my. It can't be. There must be a mistake. This is *my* baby. Mine..."

"Not anymore. Now it's *ours*."

Whether it was the shock, the heat or his alarming words, she suddenly felt faint. Black spots danced before her eyes and the room began to whirl around her. She must have swayed, because the next thing she knew he was at her side. Ignoring her cry of protest, he slid one big muscular arm around her back, slipped the other under her knees and lifted her into his arms.

If Susan hadn't already felt faint, his sudden proximity would have done it. Cradled against his broad chest, she was bombarded by foreign sensations. There was his warmth, the steely strength of his body, the solid beat of his heart against her breast. She squeezed her eyes shut, awash in contradictory feelings. Part of her wanted him to put her down this instant. But another part, shameless and unfamiliar, had an awful desire to snuggle closer. Confused, she gave a grateful sigh as he leaned over and she felt the nubby surface of her couch against the backs of her legs.

Without a word, he sat beside her and forced her head toward her knees. "Breathe," he ordered.

She nodded, doing as he said until the world quit spinning. "I'm sorry," she murmured finally, shrugging off his hand and sitting upright. "I'm not usually a fainter. It's just...I can't seem to take it in..." Swallowing, she turned to look at him. "Are you sure?"

He nodded. "Positive. I just spent an hour with Margaret Richey. There's no question. The child you're carrying is mine."

A dozen questions immediately popped into her mind. Like, why had the clinic told him before they'd told her? Wasn't there some sort of rule that she had to be notified first? As far as that went, shouldn't Mrs. Richey have come in person to tell her, instead of allowing Sterling to deliver the news?

Yet those things could all be answered later. Right now, the only question that mattered was the one she was most terrified to have answered. "Why—" she had to stop and clear her throat "—why are you here? What do you want?"

"I told you. We need to talk."

As an answer, that was hardly illuminating. She considered him, trying to read his emotions and drawing a blank. Whatever he felt, he didn't let it show on his face. He simply looked...remote. And very formidable. "I—I won't make any claim on you," she said slowly, wondering if that was at the heart of his reserve. "I mean, I know you have money, but this doesn't really have anything to do with you. It was entirely my decision and I'm more than prepared to take full responsibility—"

"No."

"Excuse me?"

"I said, no. Biologically this child is half mine. Not only do I expect to take my share of the responsibility, but—" for the first time he hesitated, if only for a second "—I'm willing to take all the responsibility."

"What do you mean?"

"I mean that if you'll give me the child, I'll see to it that it has everything it could possibly need."

She could feel her eyes widen as his meaning sank in. She jumped to her feet. "No!" Agitation stripped away the last trace of her normal reserve. "I could never do that. This is my baby! I've waited and planned and dreamed about having it, and I'm not giving it up. Not to you or anybody!"

He stared stonily at her, then leaned back on the couch and crossed his arms. "All right. We'll get married."

"What?"

"We'll get married," he repeated. "It's probably better, anyway. Kids ought to have two parents."

She'd been right earlier. He was crazy. "Don't be ridiculous. I don't even know you!"

He climbed to his feet, once again towering over her. "Then it's time you start. And what you'd better understand is, that's my kid you're carrying, most likely my son, and I'm not going to stand on the sidelines, with no say in his upbringing, while he spends most of his life either alone or with a baby-sitter while you struggle to support him. So you can either marry me—or I'll sue you for custody. Your choice. Although—'' he took a pointed look around, his gray eyes unreadable as he examined her minuscule living room with its worn furnishings ''—I think it's only fair to point out that you'd have a mighty slim chance of winning.''

Susan stared at him. It was clear from his implacable expression that he meant every word he said. Still, the whole idea was crazy. Marriage was meant to be the kind of loving, trusting relationship her parents had enjoyed, not an alternative to being sued, for heaven's sake.

Still, he was right about one thing. In the best of all possible worlds, a child should have two parents to love it. Not that she agreed with his crazy proposal. She couldn't possibly marry him. The whole idea was preposterous.

Yet his expression made it clear that he expected her to acquiesce. ''I—I'll need some time to think about it,'' she hedged instead, trying to buy herself some time until she could come up with a better solution.

His eyes narrowed. ''No. Nothing is going to change, and I don't want people counting on their fingers when our child is born. It's going to be touch and go as it is.''

''But what if something happens? It's still early in the pregnancy yet. Something could go wrong...''

''We'll deal with that if it happens.''

''Oh, but—''

''Look, I'm not exactly wild about this myself.'' For half a second, a bleak look came over his face. Then his expression hardened. "But it is the best solution. I don't know what you've heard about me, but I'm not some sort of wife beater or anything. I promise I'll take good care of you and the baby. You won't have to worry about anything."

"I'm sure that's true, but still…"

"Yes or no?" he said intractably.

"I…"

"Choose."

Oh! What should she do? Squeezing her eyes shut, she tried to envision marriage to Sterling—and failed. She had no trouble, however, picturing the two of them in court. In her mind, she could see him surrounded by high-priced lawyers as some faceless judge banged a gavel down and awarded him custody of *her* baby. "I…I—yes," she whispered.

"Good." He was suddenly brusque. "How does tomorrow sound to you?"

Her eyes popped open. "For what?"

"The ceremony. Judge Lester's a friend of mine. I'm sure he'll be glad to do it."

"But I have to work!"

"Call in and tell them you quit," he commanded. "I've got more than enough money for the both of us, and in your condition you shouldn't be on your feet anyway."

She gazed at him in shock, stunned by how casually he was rearranging her entire life. "But—but—I can't!"

"You have family you need to call? Just tell me who it is, and I'll have them flown in."

"No," she said faintly. "There's nobody."

He crossed his arms. "Then what's the holdup?"

"It's…" She tried desperately to think of an answer other than *it's too soon*, pretty certain it would get her nowhere. "I don't have anything to wear," she said lamely.

"Huh." Without another word, he reached into his pocket, pulled out a money clip, peeled off some bills and thrust them at her. "Here."

"Oh, no. I can't—"

"Take it." His gaze touched briefly on her dress, then came back to her face. "Go out and buy yourself something pretty."

"Oh, but—"

"Unless something changes, I'll come by tomorrow at twelve forty-five to pick you up."

She thought of all the things she had to do. She'd have to call her landlord, her boss and the clinic. Luckily the house had come furnished, but the refrigerator and the cupboards would still have to be cleaned out. She'd have to call to turn off her utilities. And find time to shop for a new dress. And, of course she'd have to pack...

She fought off a fresh wave of exhaustion. Taken all together, it was close to overwhelming. She was going to need every minute she had. "No. Please. I'll—I'll meet you there."

"Okay," he said reluctantly. "One o'clock, the county courthouse. The judge's chambers are on the second floor." He searched her face. He must have seen her uncertainty, because he said abruptly, "Give me your word you'll be there, Susan."

She stared back at him, stung as she saw the distrust in his eyes. "I'll be there. I promise."

"All right." With a stiff nod, he settled his hat on his head and strode toward the door, where he smacked the screen open with his palm and was gone.

Susan stared dazedly after him. Oh, dear. It appeared she was getting married.

Whether she wanted to or not.

TWO

She wasn't coming.

Sterling paced restlessly along the courthouse hall-way. Although the air was cool thanks to the air-con-ditioning, he'd managed to work up a sweat. As a result, he'd loosened his tie and tossed his navy suit coat over a corridor chair a while ago. Now, stripped down to his shirtsleeves and vest, he glanced at his wristwatch for what felt like the umpteenth time, then stalked over to glare out the bank of windows that overlooked the build-ing's main entrance.

It was 1:10 and there wasn't a redhead in sight.

"Mr. Churchill?"

He swiveled around, recognizing the voice of Judge Lester's clerk. "Yes?"

The young man hesitated. "I don't mean to worry you, but I thought I'd better mention that His Honor is due back in court at two. If your fiancée is delayed much longer, I'm afraid we'll have to reschedule."

"No problem. She should be here any minute."

Apparently he sounded more confident than he felt, because the clerk readily nodded. "Good. But as soon as she arrives, if you could come straight inside, we'll get started."

"Fine." The instant the younger man disappeared back through the door into the judge's chambers, Sterling whipped around to once more scan the sidewalk down below.

Nothing. He swore under his breath. Susan Wilkins wasn't coming and it was his own damn fault. He never should have agreed to let her get to the courthouse on her own. For that matter, he never should have let her out of his sight. His instinct—the one that had lifted him out of a childhood of near-poverty and made him a millionaire before he turned thirty—had urged him to close this deal while he could. He should have listened to it, should have heeded the inner voice of experience that had warned him that speed was of the essence.

Because, while there was no way for Ms. Wilkins to know that he would never take a child away from its mother, by now she might have figured out that a court was far more likely to order him to pay support than grant him custody.

Then again, why would she settle for half the pie when she could have it all? She'd made it clear yesterday that she knew he had money. And, though he knew his attorney was going to have a coronary when he found out, Sterling had deliberately chosen not to ask for a prenup so that by marrying him, she'd have a direct claim on his wealth—a fact he'd counted on to work in his favor.

He grimaced. It appeared he'd thought wrong. It appeared that if he had the brains God gave a Hereford, he would have called the judge from her dingy little living room yesterday and taken care of everything then and there.

Of course, he had been practically out on his feet. And there was no guarantee that the judge would've been available. Or that he could have arranged things on such short notice. Hell, he'd had to pull strings to make this happen today.

Besides, Susan *had* given him her word she'd be here—

Aw, come on, Churchill, get real. Teresa promised to love, honor and cherish you for the rest of your life and you know how that turned out. When are you going to learn?

His face tightened at the reminder of his ex-wife. Bracing his hands against the windowsill, he hunched his shoulders and stared blindly out into the bright September sun, remembering the day she'd packed up and left him. He'd spent most of their marriage trying to make up to her for the child they couldn't have. But it hadn't been until that winter afternoon four years ago that he'd finally accepted that no matter how hard he tried, he'd never be enough to fill the void in her life. It had been a bitter pill to swallow, and he'd vowed, as he stood there and watched her drive away, that he would never again open himself up to such heartbreak.

So it wasn't as if he *wanted* to get married. If it weren't for the child, there wasn't a tinker's chance in hell he'd even consider it. But there was a child on the way. And not only did he want it with every fiber of his being, but he was damned if he was going to let it grow up the way he had, with no father and a mother who was too busy putting food on the table to bother with anything else.

A flurry of motion caught his attention. Glancing to his left, Sterling watched a woman hurriedly cross the street at the far corner and head in his direction. For a second his heart sped up as he saw that she had red hair, but it only took him an instant to realize it wasn't his intended.

For one thing, instead of a dowdy auburn bun, this woman had a rich sorrel mane streaked with fiery strands of copper and chestnut that tumbled in sexy disarray past her slender shoulders.

For another, she was a real head-turner as she dashed along in a stylish lavender dress that skimmed her delicately curved body and strappy high heels that made her long, slim legs appear to go on forever.

He felt an unwanted tightening in his groin. In the next instant, he told himself firmly he was glad the woman wasn't Susan, who, if yesterday was any indication, seemed to favor clothes that would make her a contender in a Frump of the Month competition.

Not that she was repulsive or anything. She had nice enough features. And good teeth. And what he'd been able to see of her body—arms, neck, ankles and feet—had been okay. Yet she was also totally forgettable, the sort of plain, unassuming female who would fade quietly into any background.

And Sterling was grateful. Hell, he was more than grateful, he was relieved. Having to get married was bad enough. While he meant every word he'd said when he told Susan he'd take good care of her, the last thing he wanted was to have feelings for her. When it came to women, he was done with any sort of tender emotions.

"Mr. Churchill?"

It was the clerk again. With an inner sigh, he turned. "What?"

"I really am afraid that we're running out of time. We need to either get started or—"

Down the hall, the bell on the elevator *pinged* and the door slid open. Sterling glanced over, his attention momentarily arrested as the woman from the street stepped out. Clutching a small silver bag in delicate fingers, she took a hurried look around, her hair swinging around her like a fiery cloak.

Damned if something about her didn't seem faintly familiar, he thought uneasily. He shifted his gaze back to the court clerk, determined to focus on what the man was saying—

"Sterling?"

That voice. It couldn't be... He turned, his whole body going tight with disbelief.

"I'm so sorry I'm late," the vision in lavender said breathlessly, hurrying toward him. "Usually I'm right on time, but things took longer than they said at the salon, and then I couldn't get a cab, and I walked as fast as I could, but I'm not used to wearing heels..." Coming to a halt before him, she bit her full lower lip, looking uncertain as their gazes met.

He stared at her in shock. "Susan?" Thanks to a subtle application of makeup, the same features that yesterday had seemed faded and nondescript, today were anything but. Her dark brown eyes seemed huge, while the mouth that she was nervously nibbling the lipstick off appeared achingly erotic.

Judge Lester's clerk clapped his hands together, his expression relieved. "You must be Miss Wilkins." He gave Susan an approving once-over as she stood there looking both sexy and classy, a jacket that matched her dress draped stylishly over one slim, milky arm. "I'm so glad you made it. As I was just telling Mr. Churchill, we need to get started. If you'd both follow me, please?" He marched importantly toward the door.

Susan glanced uncertainly after him, then turned back to Sterling. "I truly am sorry I'm late. I hope you're not angry."

"Me? Angry? Hell, no." He reached over, snagged his coat off the chair and yanked it on. "I just figured you weren't coming."

"What?" Her eyes widened in surprise. "But I promised."

For some reason, the discovery that her word meant something to her was almost as unsettling as her incredible—and totally unwelcome—transformation. "Forget it. At least you're here now. Shall we go in?"

"Oh, but—that is, if you could give me just one second—" Her movements hurried, she handed him her ridiculously little purse, then quickly slipped on her jacket, flipped her hair free of the collar and smoothed it back with her fingers.

A faint whiff of perfume enveloped him at her movement. The scent was as soft and evocative as she looked. To his horror, it was all he could do not to lean forward, press his lips to some silky patch of her and see if she tasted as good as she looked. Wondering what the hell was wrong with him, he impatiently yanked the knot on his tie into place—and nearly strangled himself.

"There." Oblivious to his rapidly deteriorating mood, she carefully retrieved her purse from his rigid hands, took a deep breath and squared her shoulders. "I'm ready."

It's about time. He took a step, then stopped. Reaching over he snatched his hat and the small gardenia bouquet he'd brought off the chair, thrusting the latter at her. "Here. These are for you."

She looked at him in surprise, then slowly took the flowers and lifted them to her face. "Oh, Sterling, they're lovely," she breathed, her face lighting up in a way that was anything but plain. "Thank you."

"It's no big deal," he said stiffly, motioning her to precede him down the hall. She gazed up at him, her lips parting as if she were going to say something, and then she seemed to lose her nerve. Squaring her shoulders, she turned and started toward the judge's chambers.

Stubbornly resisting an unacceptable urge to check out the sway of her slender hips, Sterling took a fortifying breath and followed, his face grim.

Just for a second, he couldn't remember why this had seemed like such a good idea ten minutes ago.

"...and so, by the power vested in me by the great state of Texas, I now pronounce you husband and wife."

His official duties fulfilled, Judge Lester rocked back on his heels, clapped Sterling on the back with one beefy hand and said jovially, "You know what that means, doncha, boy? That means you can finally pucker up and kiss your pretty little bride." The jovial judge winked conspiratorially at Susan, then shifted his gaze to her husband. "Go on, now. This is no time to be shy." Eyes twinkling, he waited expectantly.

Gathering her courage, Susan snuck an apprehensive glance at Sterling. Just as she feared, his good-looking face held a complete lack of enthusiasm for the judge's suggestion.

Her spirits sank. For all his insistence that *she* marry *him,* he'd spent the past twenty minutes acting like the reluctant groom at a shotgun wedding. Curt and unsmiling, he'd suffered through introductions to the court reporter who was acting as a witness along with the clerk, and had only reluctantly made small talk with the judge. And though he'd said his vows in a clear voice without hesitation, he'd done it with all the warmth of a man reciting an arrest warrant.

It hadn't exactly been the wedding of her dreams, either, Susan acknowledged wistfully. But then, it wasn't supposed to be, she reminded herself, absently twisting the gleaming gold band on her ring finger. She was doing this for the baby. Hadn't she been awake all night, considering her options? And hadn't she decided that she wanted more for her child than a life on the run or a childhood shaped by a series of court battles?

Yes, absolutely. What's more, there were genuine benefits to marrying Sterling. As he'd pointed out, two parents were better than one. Not only would her child have two people to love it, but it would also have someone else to depend on should anything happen to her.

She also realized that Sterling's wealth was a plus. While she didn't care about the money for herself, she realized he could provide numerous advantages for their child that she couldn't—as much as it humbled her to admit it. And she couldn't deny that she was thrilled at the prospect of actually getting to stay home and be a full-time mother.

So she supposed it also shouldn't matter how Sterling felt about her.

But it did.

While she knew it was probably rather foolish of her, deep down she'd cherished the hope that he would be pleased she'd made an effort to look nice for him.

Of course, she hadn't intended to do anything quite this drastic, she acknowledged, self-consciously pressing her lipsticked lips together. When she'd hesitantly walked into Cachet first thing this morning, she'd simply hoped to find something on sale that didn't look too bad on her. She'd certainly never intended to confide to the elegant saleslady that she was getting married later that· day. Or confess that her intended was everything she was not—attractive, important, self-confident—and that she wished, for his sake, that she was just a little bit pretty. And she'd most definitely never expected the saleslady to take her statement as a personal challenge.

But the woman had. Before Susan had known it, the saleslady had whisked her into a dressing room, ordered her to strip down to her undies, then studied her with a critical eye. Murmuring to herself about delicate lines, fabulous coloring and absolutely no fashion sense, she'd disappeared, then returned with an armful of beautiful clothing. In no time at all, Susan had found herself the owner of the lilac sheath she'd admired only the day before, a matching coat, some slacks, two pair of shorts, a trio of incredibly expensive little T-shirts—and some racy new lingerie that she hadn't had the nerve to admit she probably wouldn't be needing.

She'd also found herself escorted next door to the beauty salon. Refusing to take no for an answer, the saleslady—whom by then Susan had been calling Jean-nette—had consulted with the stylist, explained what she wanted done and voilà! Two hours later, Susan had emerged several hundred dollars poorer, looking quite unlike her previous self.

She had to admit that she'd been quietly thrilled with her new look as she'd hurried along Royal's streets to-ward the courthouse. At least now Sterling won't have to be ashamed of me, she'd told herself as she recalled the pointedly reserved way he'd looked at her the previous day.

Not that she'd done it for him. She hadn't. She'd done it for herself, because she was starting a whole new chapter in her life and she wanted to put her best foot forward.

And it was good that she felt the way she did, she thought ruefully, since Sterling hadn't even seemed to notice her changed appearance.

"Susan?"

"Yes?" She glanced up, then froze as Sterling reached out, cupped her shoulders in his hands and lowered his head. Even though his intention was obvious, she was still unprepared for the foreign feel of his lips as they brushed against her cheek. Startled, she gave a little jerk of surprise and tipped her head.

Just like that they were mouth-to-mouth.

Susan drew in her breath. The last person to kiss her had been a fellow student her first year of college. He'd been no more than a boy, and it was a toss-up which of them had been more nervous and inexperienced.

But there was nothing boyish or inexperienced about her new husband. On the contrary, his lips were warm and firm, his hands were strong and steady, and his scent—the same clean, masculine one that had made her tremble on her front porch yesterday—was heavenly. The second she relaxed, she found that being kissed…by him…like this…was really quite lovely.

With an instinct she didn't question, she raised her arms and slid her hands around Sterling's neck. Her fingertips slid over the fine fabric of his suit coat, encountered the smooth cotton of his crisp white collar, then finally found the soft thickness of his hair. She hesitantly stroked it, startled as the kiss became fractionally more urgent. Intrigued, she caressed him again, feeling a shameless little thrill when he pulled her closer.

Oh, my. Who would have thought that just kissing could cause this explosion of warmth to spread through her? Or that somebody who acted as forbidding as Sterling would turn out to be such a terrific kisser?

Not her, she thought foggily. Based on their meeting yesterday, she would have sworn he was all brusque un-sentimentality. Yet that didn't explain the money he'd given her to buy a dress, or the bouquet of flowers he'd brought her, or that he'd remembered a wedding ring. Much less how he'd wound up being such a champion kisser—

Without warning, he pulled away. Caught off guard, her eyes flew open. She stared up at him, her instinctive cry of protest silenced by the chilly glitter in his gray eyes.

Susan had seen pictures of icebergs that looked warmer. Except of course for that odd flush high on his cheekbones...

"Woowee!" the judge exclaimed happily. "I surely do love a wedding! Don't you, Jimmy Lee?" he asked his clerk.

"Yes, I do, Judge," the young man agreed. "However—" he glanced pointedly at his watch "—I'm afraid that we're running shy on time. The noon recess will be over in a few minutes."

The judge sighed good-naturedly. "Then I suppose it's time I get back to work," he agreed. "Although I can't say I'm looking forward to it. That dadburn fool Rooster Roberts is back on the docket, causing trouble again..." Shaking his head, he reached out, shook Sterling's hand, then winked at Susan. "You make sure this ole boy takes good care of you, okay, darlin'? And if he doesn't, you just haul him back in here and I'll slap his butt in jail, I promise.''

Clasping her hands to keep from pressing her fingers to her tingling lips, Susan managed a tremulous smile. ''Thank you, Your Honor.''

The clerk waited as they signed the marriage certificate, handed it to Sterling, then efficiently hustled the two of them toward the door.

The next thing Susan knew, she and Sterling were alone in the hall. There was an awkward silence. For a moment she felt an attack of shyness coming on, but she forced it away. After all, she reminded herself, this was the start of a whole new life. If nothing else, she had to *try*. She forced herself to look squarely up at Sterling's handsome face. ''Well,'' she said lightly. ''That didn't take long.''

''Nope.'' He abruptly settled his hat on his head and nodded at the elevator. ''Come on. I'm parked out front.''

Okay, so he wasn't big on small talk. That was okay. She obviously wasn't, either. Things would get better as they got to know each other.

Still, she couldn't help but notice the care he took not to touch her as they stepped into the enclosed space of the elevator. And even though she knew she wasn't being fair, as the doors slid shut and the car began to drop, she couldn't deny she felt an undeniable twinge of disappointment.

Arms crossed, Sterling stood looking out Susan's screen door, his back to her small living room.

Outside, the day had turned still and hot, the sort of hazy, lazy afternoon that felt like summer except for an indefinable hint of fall in the air.

Inside, he could hear Susan moving around in the other room, putting the finishing touches on her packing. In no time at all, she was going to be done. And then she was going to walk in here and expect to go home with him.

And why not? He'd given her that right when he'd said "I do." In return, he now had exactly what he wanted—a chance to be a full-time father, to make sure that when the time came his kid would have the complete benefit of his protection.

It was a fair exchange. So why didn't he feel better?

Well, hell, that was easy. It was her. Susan. In the course of twenty-four hours, she'd gone from being so unassuming she was practically invisible, to being the sort of woman who could get under your skin if you let her.

Not that he was going to let her. Sure, the kiss they'd shared earlier in the judge's chambers may have gotten a little out of hand. But then, she'd caught him totally off guard. The last thing he'd expected was for her to respond to an obligatory buss on the cheek by twining herself around him like some fragrant clinging vine. Much less that she'd practically melt with pleasure from something as basic as an everyday, elementary, closed-mouth kiss.

But she had. And he'd been so nonplussed that for a few seconds there he'd had an inexplicable urge to clear off the judge's desk, lay her down on top of it and see what happened next.

Dammit.

Sterling shoved a hand through his hair, frustrated and a little embarrassed at the memory of his heated response. Okay. So maybe she *had* gotten to him just a little. It didn't mean a darned thing. He'd simply been knocked temporarily off balance by the startling change in her appearance and things had gone downhill from there.

But that was over. Done. In the past. He now had himself well in hand and he wasn't about to let a brief lapse in judgment ruin a perfectly good marriage of convenience. All he wanted out of this union was the right to his child. He did not want to be attracted to that child's mother. And the sooner the new Mrs. Churchill understood that, the better off they'd both be.

"Sterling?"

He turned. Susan stood just inside the interior doorway, awkwardly clutching a large Cachet box under one arm, while she held an old, mismatched suitcase in each hand. Her cheeks were flushed, her hair slightly mussed, her skin glowing from her recent exertion. It was a damn good thing he wasn't letting her get to him, he thought sourly. Because if he was he'd be forced to admit she looked good. Real good.

He indicated the bags. "That it?"

"Yes. Except for my books. And some household items, towels, linens, knickknacks, that sort of thing."

"Like I told you," he said as he closed the distance between them, took the suitcases from her and set them by the door. "I'll send one of my men over with a pickup tomorrow to get the rest of your stuff. Once you've seen my place, you'll have a better idea what you want to keep."

She nodded. "Yes. I know. Thank you."

There was a brief pause as Sterling gathered his thoughts. "There's something we need to discuss," he began.

"Oh! I almost forgot—" Susan said simultaneously.

They both fell silent. Sterling managed a terse smile. "Ladies first."

"It's nothing really," she said quickly. "That is, it is to me, but it may not be to you. It's just…about my job…"

He frowned. "I thought we agreed you were going to quit."

Inexplicably the faintest flicker of disbelief came and went on her face before she said, "Well…yes. But you see, it'll take some time for them to replace me, and I can't just leave them in the lurch that way, so I've agreed to work part-time. It'll just be for a while," she was quick to assure him. "And I did arrange to take the rest of this week off."

He supposed he couldn't fault her for being conscientious. "Okay. Is that it?"

"Actually, there is one other thing…" Her voice trailed off as she walked over and picked up her purse off the sofa. She opened it and pulled out a roll of bills. "Here." She offered the money to him.

He frowned. "What's that for?"

"It's yours. You gave it to me yesterday. Remember?"

"Yeah. So?"

"So it was very kind of you, but as it turned out, I didn't need it. I took care of things myself."

He gave her lavender dress a quick glance, staunchly trying not to notice the way it clung in strategic places to the slim body that shaped it. He might not be an expert on women's clothing, but he knew it hadn't come from the Bargain Mart. Just as a single glance around the rather shabby living room was proof enough that his bride was hardly rolling in money. Wondering what her game was, he said carefully, "Look, I expect to pay your way. Even though this isn't a conventional marriage—" it couldn't hurt to lay a little groundwork "—you're still my wife. Legally at least."

"But I wasn't yesterday," she countered earnestly. "And it just doesn't feel right to take your money. Not that I'm not grateful. It—it was very sweet and very generous of you to give it to me. But I think it's important that we start out on the right foot and I don't want you to think I'm some sort of gold digger." When he still didn't make a move to take the cash, she carefully reached out and slipped it into his coat pocket.

His lips involuntarily compressed at the jolt of awareness that shot through him at her innocent touch.

Oblivious to his discomfort, she took a few steps back, linked her hands together and smiled tentatively up at him. "Now. What did you want to tell me?"

He stared back at her. Well, shoot. What was he supposed to do now? Tell her to hell with starting off on the right foot, it would make things a whole lot easier if she was just a tad bit less ethical?

Then, at least, they could have a nice, straightforward business arrangement. Instead she was complicating everything by her insistence on being so...nice. Not that he wasn't pleased that the mother of his child appeared to have some standards, he was quick to assure himself. He was. But still...between the way she looked, the way she kissed, and now this, nothing was going the way he expected. And he didn't like it. He didn't like it at all.

On the other hand, they *did* have to live together. And it was sort of flattering—in a totally annoying way— how she'd gone to such lengths to spruce herself up for him. More important, given her delicate condition, he sure as hell didn't want to take a chance on upsetting her. Which was a distinct possibility, he realized uneasily as he gazed into her concerned brown eyes.

Damn. What if he said the wrong thing and she got hysterical and fainted or something and hurt herself or the baby?

His stomach hollowed and he came to a sudden decision. He'd lay down the law in a few days, after she'd settled in at his place. And in the interim he'd keep to himself until she got the picture. Then, when she'd had some time to accept how things stood, they'd talk.

"Sterling?" Susan said. "Did you want to say something?"

"No," he said decisively.

She worried her lower lip, then released it. "Are you sure?"

With a start of disgust, he realized his eyes were riveted on the full, soft curve of her mouth. Jerking his gaze away, he wheeled, picked up the suitcases and nudged open the screen, holding it open for her. "I'm sure. I think we ought to get going."

She hesitated, then nodded. "Okay." Taking a deep breath, she drew herself up and took one last look around the room. Then she picked up the Cachet box and her bridal bouquet and walked resolutely toward him and the door.

Stopping as she drew abreast of him, she caught him by surprise as she lightly laid a hand on his forearm. "I realize this isn't an easy situation for either of us," she said softly. "But I want you to know, I'll do my best to be a good mother to the baby and a good wife to you."

Great. Just what he wanted to hear. "Yeah. Me, too," he mumbled in return. Since he didn't mean a word of it, for a second he felt like the biggest heel on earth.

Then she nodded, glanced shyly away and set off for

the car—but not before her hip brushed against his thigh as she passed by.

His body instantly tightened.

So did his resolve. For whatever reason, there was something about her that seemed to have a disastrous effect on his self-control. And he liked *that* the least of all.

The quicker he established some distance between them, the better off they'd both be.

Three

"Oh, my," Susan said softly.

Standing beside the car, she stared at the house before her. Like everybody in the area, she'd heard about Sterling's place. She'd even driven past the ornate entrance gate once with Callie to see for herself the emerald green pastures, man-made lake and graceful groves of trees that made the lush estate such a novelty in the arid scrubland of West Texas. Not surprisingly, the locals had taken to calling it the Oasis and the name had stuck.

The house couldn't be seen from the road, however, set back as it was in a screen of trees at the end of the long, straight driveway. Secretly she'd been worried that it was going to be so imposing she'd never feel comfortable in it.

Now, some of her tension melted away. Instead of the formal, white-pillared mansion she'd expected, the structure rising before her was a big, sprawling two-story surrounded by a wild profusion of bushes and flowers. From what she could see, it was warm rather than palatial, charming rather than impressive, welcoming rather than intimidating.

It didn't seem to suit Sterling at all, she thought ruefully, watching him from under her lashes as he got her suitcases from the trunk.

So far, he'd been anything but warm and welcoming. Not only had he barely spoken a word on the drive over, but it had almost seemed as if he'd been trying to avoid looking at her. And though she'd told herself that it didn't mean a thing, that he was just being a conscientious driver, she had to admit that his aloofness was starting to get to her.

Waiting until he looked up, she bravely met his cool gray gaze. "This is lovely, Sterling."

His expression lightened for a moment. "Yeah. It's okay." Closing the trunk, he picked up her suitcases and led the way across the paved circular driveway and up the wide, shallow stairs to a trellised entryway. Overhead, a leafy vine abloom in white flowers gave off a faintly spicy perfume.

Captivated, Susan again tried to start up a conversation. "Oh, how pretty. Is that a clematis?"

He set down the suitcases and reached to open the door. "Beats me. You'll have to ask Maxine."

"Maxine?"

"My housekeeper." His voice took on a distinctly sardonic tone. "She likes to think she knows everything."

"Oh." Susan felt a pang of dismay. While she was relieved to discover that they weren't going to be all alone in the house, she didn't know a thing about having hired help. Heavens, she'd never even had a cleaning lady. What if this Maxine didn't like her?

She didn't have to wait long to find out. She'd barely crossed the threshold before a tall, energetic woman dressed in trim white slacks and a bright turquoise blouse materialized at the end of the hall. "Well, I declare, it's about time you two got here," the newcomer drawled with a pronounced Texas twang as she marched purposefully closer. "I was startin' to worry. I put the last touch on the cake half an hour ago."

Sterling's eyes narrowed. "What cake?"

The woman, who appeared to be in her fifties, and who had shrewd brown eyes, a weathered face and improbable blond hair swept up in the sort of elegant chignon that Susan could never achieve, smiled at him blandly. "Why, your weddin' cake, boss. You didn't think I'd let something as important as your gettin' hitched pass without at least fixin' you a special dinner, did you?"

Blithely ignoring his obvious lack of enthusiasm, she shifted her focus. "You must be Susan," she said warmly. "Why, aren't you a pretty little thing! The boss never said a word about that, but then, he wouldn't." She flashed her employer a brief, reproachful look, then brightened. "But I guess I'm gettin' the cart before the horse. I'm Maxine, and I take care of most of the important things around here. I'm sure this must all seem a tad overwhelmin' at the moment, what with the baby and this quickie marriage, but you just wait and see, you'll be settled in no time.

"Now, why don't you let me show you your room, and then you can see the rest of the house. I'll get one of the boys to bring up your suitcases later, unless you need something right away."

Susan glanced at Sterling, feeling a bit dazed. Unless she'd missed something, it appeared he'd explained their situation to his housekeeper. While she didn't mind exactly—when she stopped to think about it she could see that anything else would have raised all sorts of awkward questions—he could at least have warned her.

Yet conversing with her was clearly not high on his list of priorities. "You go ahead," he said, his expression once again impossible to read. "I need to call my office."

"Yeah, and you need to call your lawyer," Max informed him tartly. She made a sour face. "I'm tellin' you, for such a supposed hotshot, that man is plenty excitable. He's called here three times, babblin' about some message you left on his answering machine and insistin' he has to talk to you."

"Great," Sterling murmured. "Anything else?"

"As a matter of fact, yessir there is. Greg Hunt called. Said he had some information for you about that immigrant you and some of the other gentlemen from the Cattleman's Club are sponsoring and that he'd appreciate it if you'd give him a call."

"Terrific." With a stiff nod, he walked down the hall and disappeared around the corner.

Susan stared after him, telling herself to give him the benefit of the doubt. Rather than being deliberately rude, he probably just hadn't adjusted his thinking yet to include a wife. Once he did, he'd no doubt be appalled at his thoughtlessness in practically abandoning her at the front door.

As if reading her mind, Maxine laid a hand on her shoulder and urged her toward the sweeping staircase that curved up to the second floor. "Don't mind him, darlin'," she said breezily. "The first thing you gotta know about the boss is that beneath all that growl, the man's a cupcake. Not—'' she rolled her eyes ''—that he'd ever admit it, you understand.''

"Of course not,'' Susan murmured, despite the fact that in the short time she'd known Sterling, the word cupcake had never, ever, entered her mind in regard to him. But then again, she really didn't know him, she reminded herself yet again as she followed Maxine down an open, airy hallway and through a door that opened to the left.

"Oh, my,'' she said for the second time in ten minutes. The room—her bedroom, she realized—was beautiful. It was decorated in soft shades of blue, white and yellow. Like the rest of the house that she'd seen so far, it was also light and airy. It had a high ceiling, cream-colored walls, gleaming white wood molding, and a pale wood floor covered with a gorgeous Oriental rug.

There was a queen-size bed, a beautiful cherrywood chiffonier and matching dresser, while a sitting room area boasted a couch, tables and a lovely easy chair set before a small, marble fireplace. Windows ran the length of one wall, overlooking the back of the house. Down below was a pool and an enormous patio. There was a sweep of green lawn that was bordered by a white railed fence. Inside, a dozen glossy-coated horses industriously cropped grass.

"Pretty room, isn't it?'' Maxine said cheerfully. "My daughter Dorrie decorated it. It was her thank-you to Sterling for putting her through design school.''

Susan smoothed her hand over the plush satin comforter, digesting that bit of information. "She's obviously very talented. Is she your only child?''

"Lord, no! There's Carter, he's a lawyer, and my twins, Gene and Lon, who both went into engineering.

Then comes Phyllis, who just got her teaching degree, and then Dorrie. She's the baby.''

"What an accomplished group. You must be very proud of them.''

"Oh, I am. They're not only good people, they're all doin' real well. Of course, part of that last is due to the boss, since he insisted on payin' their way through school.'' She chuckled. "But then, I'm sure you don't want to be hearin' about that. Get me started on all the good that man does and we could be here the rest of the day.''

"We could?''

"Oh, absolutely,'' the housekeeper confirmed. "You can hardly make a move without trippin' over one of his special projects.''

"Like what?'' Susan knew it was impolite to gossip, but she couldn't stop the question.

"Well…'' Maxine considered a moment, then brightened. "See those horses out there?'' She gestured toward the windows. "Old and retired, every dad-blamed one. The boss takes them in and makes sure they get first-rate care, seeing to it they live out their lives in comfort.'' She shook her head. "Like I said, he's a good man. He'll be a wonderful daddy,'' she assured Susan, with sudden fervor. "You just wait and see.''

As if embarrassed by her outburst, she suddenly turned brusque. "Now, let me show you the layout here. That—'' she pointed at a door set in the wall to the left of the bed ''—is to the walk-in closet, while this—'' she opened a door barely noticeable in the creamy paneling ''—leads into the bathroom.''

Susan dutifully walked over and glanced in, feeling like Cinderella getting a tour of the palace as she looked around at the lavish space. Past a mirrored dressing area, a set of double doors were open to a gleaming white marble floor. There was a long black granite counter with two sinks and gleaming gold fixtures and another door that she assumed led to the toilet. A curving glass-block wall provided privacy for an etched glass shower enclosure and a huge oval tub big enough for five people.

Maxine padded across the thick pile of the carpet and opened a door set in the opposite wall. "This place was built by a transplanted Englishman," she explained. "I guess connected bedrooms are some sort of British thing 'cuz as you can see, this opens onto the boss's."

"Ah," Susan said, trying not to sound as daunted as she felt at the discovery that he was going to be so close—or that she was expected to share a bathroom with him. Grateful all over again that she wasn't suffering from morning sickness, she joined Maxine and looked around. His room was twice the size of hers, was furnished in navy and white with a touch of burgundy and had a similar view. She couldn't help the thought that it was unabashedly masculine—just like him.

"I could've put you across the hall," Maxine said as she shut the door and led the way back into Susan's room. "But you two *are* married and there's nothing like a little proximity to help two people get better acquainted, if you know what I mean." She sent Susan a knowing smile. "Besides, like I told the boss, this way the gals who come to clean once a week won't have anything to talk about. Now, I'll give you a few minutes to freshen up. Then we should have just enough time that I can show you the rest of the place before supper."

"Supper?" Susan's stomach immediately rumbled at the mention of food. When she stopped to think about it, she realized that she hadn't eaten all day. Dismayed for the baby's sake, she said gratefully, "That sounds wonderful."

Maxine smiled. "Good. I'll just run down to check on the roast and then I'll be back up to take you on that tour. Is there anything you need before I go?"

Susan hesitated. "Actually," she said, crossing to the bed where she'd set her things and picking up her wedding bouquet, "do you think you could put this in the refrigerator? Sterling got it for me and I—I'd like to enjoy the flowers just a little while longer." She knew it was probably a silly request, but they were so pretty...

"I'd be glad to, honey." Maxine took the ribbon-wrapped gardenias from her hand and made a *tsking* sound, her eyes suddenly misting. "That man," she said softly as she headed for the door. "He tries to fight it, but at heart he's just a big ole romantic."

Suzanne wasn't sure she believed that. Yet it was nice to hear all the same. She wasn't sure why, exactly. Maybe it was because Maxine seemed like such a normal, levelheaded human being. If she was convinced Susan's new husband was such a prince, how bad could he really be?

As she picked up her purse and started toward the bathroom, Susan realized only time would tell.

Sterling stood at the back fence in the gathering dusk, stroking Cassandra's silky forehead. As the leggy mare leaned into him, he felt some of his tension fade away.

This was his favorite time of day. It always seemed there was one magical moment as the sun slowly sank over the horizon when the breeze subsided and the birds fell silent and everything went still in anticipation of the approaching night.

"Boss? Dinner's ready!"

Everything but Maxine, he corrected, grimacing as the mare gave a startled jerk at the housekeeper's bellowed summons.

With a sigh of resignation, he straightened. This dinner might be the very last thing he wanted, but there was no way short of outright rudeness to avoid it. And now that he'd had some time to compose himself, he was confident he could handle it. They were merely going to share a meal, after all. What could possibly happen?

"Boss? Come on!"

He handed Cassie one last section of apple, gave her velvety nose a final stroke and pushed away from the fence. Ignoring the mare's whiffle of protest, he strode across the back lawn toward the flagstone terrace that stretched the length of the house, ending in a series of shallow steps that led down to the swimming pool.

Susan, he saw, was already seated at the patio table. She'd changed into a pair of close-fitting brown slacks and a soft, apricot-colored top. The colors looked great with her fair skin and gleaming, shot-with-fire hair. As he made a quick trip to the cabana to wash up, he found himself wondering exactly what had happened to her between the time he'd proposed and the time she'd shown up for the wedding. Whatever it was, he wished she'd knock it off. Looking at her was…distracting.

Yeah? So don't look.

It was good advice. Unfortunately it was also totally unrealistic, since the first thing she did when he dropped into the padded chair across from her was look up, fix her big brown eyes on him and smile her self-effacing smile. "Hi."

Only a total bastard wouldn't respond. Since he wasn't quite that far gone, he nodded at her. "'Evening." He settled his napkin on his lap, relieved as Maxine bore down on them carrying a large tray.

The older woman set it on the table with a clatter. "Well, even if I do say so myself, you two are in for a treat. It's not every day that I go to all the trouble to fix my special beef tenderloin with all the trimmings. And tonight it's turned out perfect."

"It smells divine," Susan said as Maxine handed her a loaded plate.

"She's right," Sterling agreed with a glance at the thinly sliced roast beef, grilled potatoes and rainbow assortment of fruits and melons on his own plate. "But it would taste a whole lot better if you'd turn off that racket," he added, referring to the passionate ballad that had begun to pour from the outside stereo speakers a few minutes earlier.

"But I like it," the housekeeper protested, her expression serene as she set a basket of rolls and a pitcher of iced tea on the table. "Music is good for the soul."

He glanced pointedly at the candles that flickered romantically in the center of the table, letting her know that he knew what she was trying to do and he didn't appreciate it. "So is being employed."

To his disgust, Maxine just laughed. "I'll turn it down, boss," she said as she sauntered away. "But that's all."

"Yeah, you do that," he said to her departing back.

Abruptly aware of the relative silence, he glanced over to find Susan watching him, an indecipherable look on her face. She said nothing however, and the moment passed as they turned their attention to the food.

Around them, the twilight was deepening, while overhead stars were beginning to appear. And though they made small talk during the meal, it wasn't until Maxine returned, served the cake and announced she was getting ready to leave for the evening that their conversation touched on anything personal.

"So…did you get your business taken care of?" Susan asked, idly stroking her thumb against her iced tea glass.

"More or less."

The call into his main office had been routine. The call to his attorney had been less so. As expected, the man had been horrified he hadn't gotten a prenup. And when Sterling had pointed out that he didn't give a damn about the money, that he could always make more, he could've sworn he heard the lawyer gnashing his teeth.

His call to Greg Hunt hadn't been nearly as satisfying. Apparently Greg's call to him had been to let him know that Princess Anna and her son were safely set up in an apartment off Main Street. And that he'd gone ahead with his plan to hide the princess in plain sight by having her work at a local café. While Sterling still wasn't wild about the idea—if it had been left up to him he would have made sure that the princess was shown every luxury—he hadn't argued about it, figuring that Greg must know what he was doing.

Besides, at the moment he was preoccupied with a certain little redheaded problem of his own.

He cleared his throat. "Did Maxine show you around?"

"Yes. It's such a beautiful house, Sterling. And the grounds, all this green… I have to confess, I'm finding it hard to believe I'm really going to live here."

She wasn't the only one. "Yeah, well…you'll get used to it."

"I guess." Leaving her cake uneaten, she yawned and

tucked her legs beneath her, settling deeper into the chair. "Have you been here long?"

He stifled a surge of impatience. Even though he would prefer not to talk about himself, he understood her curiosity. After all, they were going to have a child together. "Almost four years." He hesitated, then added reluctantly, "I had a place in Pine Valley—" he named Royal's most exclusive enclave, a gated community of mostly Georgian mansions "—but I sold it after my divorce."

She was silent. He braced, certain she was going to ask about his previous marriage, only to be pleasantly surprised as she changed the subject. "Did you grow up around here?"

"Pretty much." Relaxing a little more—this was nothing he couldn't handle—he moved his chair back from the table and stretched out his legs. "I'm from Midland."

"Oh?" Susan absently tucked a shiny lock of hair behind her ear. In the flickering candlelight, her skin looked as smooth and creamy as the finest porcelain. "Do you still have family there?"

"No. I never knew my dad, he was long gone before I was born. There's only my mom, and she lives in Florida now."

"Does she know about the baby?"

"No. Not yet." He didn't add that since he'd bought his mother a house in Miami and provided her with a generous retirement fund, he rarely heard from her. Or that she probably wouldn't care about the baby one way or another, since she'd never been particularly interested in children—hers or anyone else's. No reason to bore Susan with the family skeletons tonight. He took a sip of iced tea. "What about you? Where are you from?"

"Me?" She said it as if it hadn't occurred to her he might have questions of his own.

"That's right." He didn't try to keep the dry note from entering his voice. "It's pretty obvious from the way you talk you're not from around here."

"I suppose it is, at that," she said with a quick, unexpected smile. "I'm from Oregon. Like you, I'm an only child." She was silent a moment, then added, "I lost my parents in a car accident my sophomore year of college."

It wasn't what he expected. "I'm sorry. That must've been tough."

"It was, but it's been nine years and after a while, most of the hurt goes away. Mostly, it's just…lonely."

He looked at her sharply, surprised by her statement and by a fleeting sense of affinity. If there was one thing he knew about, it was loneliness. Sometimes, he felt as if he'd been alone all of his life.

Not that he had any intention of saying so. Instead he took another sip of his drink, set down the glass and said, "Is that why you decided to have a baby?"

The question seemed to startle her. "Because I was lonely?" She considered a moment, then answered decisively. "No."

"Then why?"

"I just always wanted a family. Mine was so happy, and growing up I always expected that someday I'd have children of my own."

"Even without a husband?" He didn't try to hide his opinion of that.

She gave a faint, good-natured sigh. "I'm twenty-eight years old and work in the Royal Library. No one was exactly breaking down my door. I guess—" her voice once again grew thoughtful "—I guess I was afraid that if I waited much longer, I'd wake up one day and it would be too late altogether.''

He felt another unexpected tug of kinship as he thought briefly about the void he'd felt in his own life recently. "I see."

She was silent a moment. "What about you? I mean, I understand that the lab messed up, but given how you feel, why did you decide to become a donor?"

"I didn't," he said flatly, hating to explain but knowing she had a right to ask. "My wife—my first wife—couldn't conceive. We went to the Clinic for help."

There was another long silence before she said quietly, "I'm sorry. That must have been difficult."

There was no curiosity in her voice, just empathy, and for a second he had an inexplicable urge to tell her the whole story. Sanity returned almost instantly, however. Glad for the darkness that hid his expression, he scowled, struck afresh by the thought that she was not what he'd expected. And by the disturbing realization that if he wasn't careful, the unfortunate effect she had on his libido could be the least of his problems.

Not that she'd gotten to him tonight. She hadn't—despite what had just almost happened. There was a simple explanation, and it was that the last four weeks had been stressful. He was tired. When you added that to the fact that he'd been working too hard the past few years to have much in the way of a love life, it also explained his earlier difficulty and why his body had…overreacted.

But it wouldn't happen again. He'd never been the sort of man to be ruled by either impulse or his physical passions, and he wasn't about to start now.

"Sterling?"

He tensed. "What?"

"I just wondered—" she paused to cover her mouth

as another yawn overtook her ''—what is it you do exactly?''

Abruptly he relaxed, once more on safe and solid ground. ''You sure you really want to hear about that?''

''Yes.''

Although he knew it was probably juvenile, he couldn't deny there was a part of him that was flattered by her interest. ''I guess I'm what you'd call a kind of venture capitalist. I invest in people or businesses that have ideas that conventional banks deem too high risk.''

''Goodness. How did you ever get started doing that?''

''I did a stint in the military, and that helped some with college, so I was able to save some money. A man I knew, a rancher I'd worked for in high school, had an idea for a new, low-cost, high-efficiency windmill. When he couldn't get financing, I gave him my savings in return for a share of future profits. The thing hit—that's his design that's pumping water out by the lake—and we both made money. That got me started and now I have interests in all sorts of things.''

''Gosh,'' Susan said softly, sounding genuinely impressed.

Overhead a star streaked across the midnight blue bowl of the sky. He heard her draw in her breath when it was followed by a second, and then a third, signaling the start of a meteor shower.

They both fell silent as they gazed at the spectacle overhead. The wind picked up slightly, setting off some wind chimes Maxine had hung beneath the eaves. By the time Sterling reluctantly looked away, he was surprised to find that his watch showed it was already half past nine. Clearing his throat, he glanced over at Susan. ''You about ready to go in?''

She didn't answer. "Susan?" Narrowing his eyes, he studied her as best he could in the darkness and, as the candlelight shifted, finally saw that her eyes were closed, her body still and relaxed.

It didn't take a genius to realize she was asleep.

He considered his options. He supposed he could fetch a blanket, cover her up and simply leave her there. Of course, if he did he really *would* qualify as a first-class bastard.

He swallowed a sigh. Climbing to his feet, he closed the short distance between them and gave her a gentle shake, determined not to notice how soft and warm she felt beneath his fingertips. "Susan?"

Her eyelids slowly lifted. "Hmm?"

"Come on." He gave her a moment, then tugged her carefully upright. "I'll walk you into the house."

"I'm sorry," she said, yawning. "I guess I fell asleep. Sometimes lately I can't seem to keep my eyes open. I just get so tired…"

"No problem." Or at least it wouldn't be if she'd just hold still. Instead she swayed unsteadily on her feet. With a sinking feeling, he realized she was still far from wide-awake. "Here. Take my arm."

"'Kay." She leaned against his arm. Then, to his dismay, she just kept on going, until she was propped bonelessly against the curve of his body. "Thanks," she said drowsily, her hand clutching the small of his back for balance.

He took a few careful steps, swearing under his breath as she unsteadily kept pace, bumping against him from armpit to thigh with every step.

Well, damn. At this rate, it would take them all night to get in the house. Either that, or they'd fall flat on their faces and never make it at all.

Neither prospect was attractive. Particularly given the way his body was reacting. So much for his vaunted control, he thought sarcastically, fighting a primitive urge to turn, bury his face in her neck, drink in her scent and press himself fully against her soft, warm curves.

He stopped walking abruptly. "Susan?"

"Hmm?"

"This isn't working."

"Oh."

"Hold still." Before he could change his mind, he turned and scooped her into his arms.

Unfortunately, unlike yesterday she didn't stiffen, even for an instant. Instead she gave a faint sigh and nestled closer, her cheek resting trustingly against the curve of his shoulder. "Sterling?" she murmured, her breath tickling against his neck.

"What?"

"Thanks."

Gritting his teeth, he set off for the house, vowing with every step that he was going to learn from this mistake.

From now on, there'd be no more candlelit dinners, no more moonlight talks, no more...touching. Instead he'd stick to his plan and give her a wide berth.

She might be the mother of his child, but that was all.

As for the unexpected twinge of protectiveness he felt as he looked down at her sleeping face...

It didn't mean a thing.

Four

Some women were just naturally beautiful first thing in the morning.

Unfortunately she wasn't one of them, Susan thought ruefully, staring at herself in the bathroom mirror.

As often happened, her impossibly slippery hair had escaped its bedtime ponytail and was tumbled wildly around her face. Her cheek sported a pillow crease, while her eyelids were still heavy from sleep. Why, even the cornflower blue top of her baby doll pajamas was askew, exposing one pale white shoulder.

She shook her head in resignation. So much for the rumored pregnancy glow. She looked like she'd been caught by one of the West Texas whirlwinds that often tore across the open range.

Not that she was complaining, she reflected, touching a hand to her still-flat stomach. She didn't care what she looked like as long as she had a healthy baby. And things could be worse. At least she didn't have to worry about anyone seeing her in this condition. Maxine never ventured upstairs until midmorning. As for Sterling, she'd barely seen him long enough to say more than a quick "hello" since they'd had dinner that first evening. He'd been on his way out when she'd come downstairs the next morning, had worked late that night, then repeated the pattern yesterday.

Straightening her pajama top, she acknowledged a slight sense of disappointment. On the one hand, she realized he had a multimillion-dollar empire to run. And that given the suddenness of their marriage, it probably wasn't fair to expect him to take time off from work, particularly since Maxine had told her that he'd just gotten back from a spur-of-the-moment trip to Europe.

Yet at the same time, he didn't seem to mind not seeing her—and that bothered her. It was also rather perplexing, since she'd been under the impression that dinner on Wednesday night had gone very well. Although she'd been nervous, she'd enjoyed the evening and had thought Sterling had enjoyed it, too. Why, by the time they'd looked up to watch that flurry of shooting stars, she'd believed they were finally off to a good start.

Apparently she'd been wrong.

If only she hadn't fallen asleep, she thought with a mixture of guilt and regret as she picked up a hairbrush and began the laborious task of wrestling her hair back into a ponytail. While honesty forced her to admit she'd enjoyed being carried into the house securely cradled in Sterling's strong arms, her common sense told her that nodding off in a man's company on your first night together probably wasn't the best way to endear yourself to him.

Not that she wanted to endear herself to Sterling. She

didn't, she was quick to assure herself. Any more than she expected that they were going to have a conventional marriage—at least, not at first.

What she did expect was for them to make an effort to get to know each other. And not because she had some impossibly naive hope that they'd fall madly in love with each other, either. No, she wanted to get better acquainted with Sterling for the sake of their child. After all, what sort of homelife would their baby have if its parents were no more than polite strangers?

The answer to that was obvious, she thought, as she finished brushing her teeth and dampened a washcloth to scrub her face. It was also unacceptable. She wanted what was best for this child, and that was to have parents who were friends and allies—if not more.

Of course, whether or not that was going to happen was another thing entirely, she admitted as, toilette complete, she rinsed out the washcloth and hung it on the towel rack. Sterling might take in old horses and remember to buy flowers and, if Maxine were to be believed, do all sorts of other kind and charitable things, but that didn't make him easy to know. On the contrary, it seemed to Susan that he was very private, rather guarded, and more than a little alone. How she was going to get past that guard remained an unknown.

It was obvious she couldn't depend on animal attraction, she decided with a wistful smile as she regarded herself in the mirror. Not unless he turned out to be interested in skinny, big-eyed women with too much hair.

Shaking her head—just once it would be kind of nice to be regarded as a sex object—she padded over and opened the door, only to gasp as she found herself face-to-face with Sterling.

"Oh!" Unnerved, she clapped a hand to her chest. "You startled me!"

"Sorry." His polite but distant tone suggested he was in no mood to chat. And on some level she supposed that was understandable, given that she was blocking his access to the facilities.

Still, she remained rooted in place. And though she tried to tell herself it was because he was standing directly in her path, she knew that was only an excuse.

The real reason she didn't move was that she was so preoccupied with staring she couldn't remember how to. And *that* was because all Sterling had on was a pair of low-slung navy pajama bottoms.

She swallowed, trying to get her stunned brain to function. Yet as she eyed his bare, bronzed chest, all she could think was that for a man who worked in an office, he certainly had a lot of muscles. "I didn't expect to see you," she heard herself babble. "I just assumed you'd left for work already."

"It's Saturday."

"Oh. Of course. I didn't think." The understatement of the century. Yet at the same time her mind was racing as she suddenly wondered what it would feel like to touch him. Would his skin be as taut and smooth as it looked? Would the vee of fine black hair that stretched between his collarbones and narrowed to a thin black line that streaked downward be soft or crinkly? She swallowed as her whole body seemed to flush. "I... I didn't wake you, did I?"

"No."

"Oh, good. That's good." Through a supreme effort of will, she dragged her gaze away from the washboard ripple of his stomach. Unfortunately she was just in time to see his gaze flick over her, reminding her with an uncomfortable jolt that he wasn't the only one who was underdressed. "I suppose you'd like me to get out of your way," she said self-consciously.

"That'd be nice." He stepped back to let her pass.

Susan took the hint. "No problem." She started forward. "I'll see you later then."

"Yeah. Sure."

To her surprise, he sounded almost surly. Even so, she managed a smile, trying to appear nonchalant as every little hair on her body tingled with electric awareness as she brushed past him.

Thankfully she didn't have to go more than a few feet before she heard the door bang shut—which was a darn good thing because her knees felt incredibly weak. She rocked to a halt, wondering what on earth was the matter with her.

After all, it wasn't as if she'd never seen a man's bare chest before. She had. Lots of times. And just because they'd all been pictures in books from the library, that didn't mean a thing. One bare chest was the same as another.

Really? Then why are you hyperventilating?

She wasn't, she told herself as she struggled to slow her ragged breathing. It was just…she wasn't a morning person. Plus she was still getting used to her new surroundings. And, given the direction of her earlier thoughts, she'd been understandably nonplussed when she'd opened that door and found Sterling standing half-naked smack-dab in front of her. All she needed were a few seconds to catch her breath and gather her composure and she'd be as good as new…

In the other room, she heard the shower come on. Out of nowhere, she had a sudden image of the stranger who was her husband shucking off his clinging pajama bottoms and stepping beneath the pounding spray. She envisioned water beading his face, running in transparent rivulets down his strong shoulders and sculptured pecs, sheeting his flat stomach and cascading onto his big, muscular thighs...

Oh, *my*.

Heat suffused her cheeks and she bolted for her bedroom, hastily slamming the connecting door behind her. Making her way to the couch, she collapsed bonelessly onto the cushions.

All right. So she'd been lying to herself. Sterling's chest *wasn't* like all the others. And there *was* a big difference between real life and a picture book. What's more, she'd been caught totally unprepared for her reaction to it. But then, how could she have imagined that sudden, powerful longing to touch him that had come over her? Or known that the sight of his bare skin would make her feel hot, shaky, confused and needy all at the same time?

She couldn't. Yet that was no reason to act like some giddy, goggle-eyed teenager. She was twenty-eight, had a degree in library science, was an expectant mother for heaven's sake!

Besides, she'd just been handed an opportunity, she realized, slowly sitting upright. As Sterling had pointed out, it was Saturday—and presumably even tycoons took the weekend off. Surely Sterling would have some free time today—some of which they might be able to spend getting to know each other better. All she had to do was screw up her courage and ask.

But first, she had to stop having these sexual thoughts about him. It was one thing to find him attractive, another to allow her imagination to run wild the way she just had. Given that Sterling didn't show the slightest sign of interest in her in return, there was simply too much at stake to allow her vivid romantic fantasies to get out of hand.

They were married. They were going to be parents. Hopefully they could learn to be friends—and *that* had to be her first priority. Which meant that from now she had to conduct herself like a grown-up. She had to be composed, forthright and self-possessed.

She took a deep breath. She could do it, she told herself firmly, lifting her chin. She could. All she had to remember was that she wasn't doing it for herself. She was doing it for the baby's sake.

With that thought staunchly in mind, she went to dress.

Sterling tensed at the soft knock on his bedroom door. He didn't need to glance at his watch to know it was way too early for his caller to be Maxine, who only worked half days on Saturday. "Who is it?" he called, even though the answer was obvious.

"Susan."

Terrific. A vision of the way she'd looked in the bathroom earlier—all soft curves and long legs—flashed through his mind. He pushed it away. "I'll be with you in a minute."

"Okay."

He finished buttoning his shirt. Then, shoving his shirttail into his jeans as he went, he strode to the door and opened it. "What can I do for you?"

"Oh— Hi. I was just wondering…" Her voice trailed off and her eyes went wide, zeroing in on his waistband.

He tried to decide what her problem was. Glancing down, he got an answer as he realized his hand was still in his pants arranging things. He froze, only to find as the seconds ticked past that her attention was having a totally unwanted effect on him. Jolted, he hastily yanked up his zipper while he still could. "You were wondering what?" he demanded.

Susan's gaze shot to his face. She stared blankly at him. "Oh! If I could speak to you," she said finally, color blooming in her cheeks.

"Yeah, I guess so. Come on in." He strode back across the room and ducked into the walk-in closet, damned if he was going to be embarrassed. "I've got some business to take care of, but I can spare you a few minutes," he told her as he reemerged with his boots. It wasn't really a lie. If he wanted to arrange for lunch and a poker game with some of the guys at the Cattleman's Club, he needed to get on it before everyone had made plans for the day.

Her face fell. "Oh."

"There a problem?" One after the other, he slid his feet into the ornately tooled leather boots, then stamped down on the heels.

"No. Not a problem. I mean, not exactly. I just thought—that is, I hoped—" She broke off. Taking a calming breath, she sent him an apologetic smile, and tried again. "I wondered if we could spend some time together today," she said hopefully, fixing her big brown eyes on him.

Well, he'd asked for it. He shook his head. "Sorry. Like I said, I'm on my way out."

"Perhaps I could go with you—"

"No. Sorry. It won't work."

"All right." She considered a moment. "Maybe we could get together later, then? I could fix dinner and—"

"No. It's real nice of you to offer, but I don't know

CAROLINE CROSS   67

how late I'll be. I'd hate to put you to all that trouble
and then get hung up.''

''Oh. Well, perhaps we could make plans for tomorrow.''

''' Fraid not.'' He scooped his wallet off the dresser
and slid it into his back pocket. ''I'm booked pretty solid
for the next few days.''

She bit her lip, considered him, then seemed to come
to some sort of decision. ''Perhaps I'm way off base,''
she said carefully, ''but if this is about what happened
Wednesday night, I apologize. I didn't mean to offend
you. I really enjoyed talking to you, and I never intended
to fall asleep, much less that you'd have to carry me into
the house—''

''I know that,'' he said sharply, stung that she'd think
he was so petty he'd hold something like that against
her. Even if he did, though not in the way she meant.
But then, he could hardly tell her that it was his libido,
not his ego, that was the problem, could he? Much less
that he couldn't forget—or forgive—that inexplicable
burst of tenderness he'd felt there at the end.

He picked up his car keys, abruptly out of patience.
''Look,'' he said gruffly, ''forget Wednesday night,
okay? It was no big deal.''

She nodded, but he could see she didn't believe him.
Still, she managed to dredge up a game little smile. ''Of
course. I don't know what made me think…'' She swallowed. ''I'm sorry. It must be hormones. I don't seem
to be quite myself lately.''

''Like I said, it's no big deal.''

''But it is,'' she contradicted. ''I've been giving it a
lot of thought, and I want our baby to be happy. Don't
you?''

Although he was damned if he understood her logic, that last was a no-brainer. "Sure."

"Then don't you think we owe it to ourselves to get to know each other? So that by the time the baby comes, we're at least comfortable with each other?"

Fat chance of *that* happening, he thought instantly. Yet as soon as he gave the question some actual thought, he had to admit she had a point.

Because unlike his own mother, Susan seemed to feel there was more to being a parent than merely providing food and shelter. And it was a pretty good hunch she wasn't going to disappear into her room and stay there once she gave birth. Like it or not, he was going to have to deal with her—one way or another.

So why hadn't this occurred to him before?

The minute he stopped to think about it the answer was obvious. He'd been so focused on his immediate goals, on securing his rights and not letting her get to him, that he hadn't thought about the future beyond his vow that things would be better for his child than they had been for him.

Yet he could suddenly see that in order to do that, it might help to be on more than just speaking terms with the kid's mother.

Not that he had to do it this instant, he temporized. He and Susan had nearly seven months before they became a family. There was no reason to rush things.

"Look, you've got a point," he said, pleased at how reasonable he sounded. "We probably do need to get better acquainted. But I just can't do it today, okay? Give me some time to clear my schedule and then we'll sit down and make some plans."

Her shoulders slumped. Yet he had to give her credit; while clearly disappointed, she didn't pout. "Of course.

Whatever you say." She took a step back toward the door. "I guess I'd better clear out so you can get going. I'll see you later." Conjuring up a smile that didn't come close to reaching her eyes, she turned and hurried out the door.

Sterling frowned. He knew it was ridiculous, but his triumph suddenly seemed sort of hollow. As a matter of fact, he felt a lot like a bully who'd just kicked a puppy.

He tried to shrug it off, telling himself it was Susan's own fault. If she'd just left him alone, given him some space instead of showing up and making demands, everything would've been fine.

But no. She'd had to press the issue. First she'd disrupted his morning by sashaying out of the bathroom and staring at him as if she'd never seen a man before. Then she'd followed it up by claiming she'd like to spend time with him.

Yeah, no wonder you're pissed. What an injustice. Not only does your not so plain Jane wife apparently find you attractive, but she's actually got the gall to want to get to know you. What diabolical thing will she think of next?

He reached up and tried to rub away some of the tension that was suddenly pinching his neck. Okay. When you put it like that, maybe he was being a little unreasonable. It probably wasn't fair to lay all the blame at Susan's door. But so far this wasn't turning out to be much of a marriage of convenience, dammit. Not when he felt under siege in his own house.

He just hadn't expected her to be so...here. Yet in a mere four days she'd made her presence felt in a host of small ways. Her razor and shampoo were in his shower. Her hairbrush and makeup decorated the bathroom counter. Her books had sprouted up like mushrooms all over the house, while her scent seemed permanently lodged in his head. Hell, he'd even found her swimsuit hanging next to his in the cabana when he'd gone for a midnight swim.

Besides, it wasn't as if he was trying to hurt her. This whole thing had just happened so fast he was still trying to get his bearings.

Yet as he started down the hall, he found he couldn't forget the forlorn look that had been on her face when she'd left his room.

He sighed. He supposed it couldn't hurt to check on her, just to make sure she was feeling all right.

Before he could change his mind, he stopped, backtracked and knocked, wondering what the hell he was going to say.

After a longish pause, the door finally opened. Susan looked out, clearly surprised to see him. "I thought you'd be gone by now." Although she smiled, her eyes were suspiciously red-rimmed.

"I'm on my way." To his relief, inspiration struck. "I just wanted to let you know I'm taking the truck, so if you want to use the Caddy to go shopping or something, you're welcome to it."

"Oh."

"The keys are in the kitchen, hanging by the door."

"Thanks."

"No problem." He glanced at his watch and told himself he really should get going. "So, what do you think you'll do today?"

She shrugged. "I don't know. I suppose I'll read."

"Huh." Not that it was any of his business, but it didn't sound too inspiring. And now that he stopped to think about it, he didn't particularly like the thought of her here all alone. What if something happened?

"Maybe you could call a girlfriend and go out to lunch."

She nodded politely. "Maybe."

They regarded each other, the seconds spinning out before Susan conjured up another strained smile. "Well, thanks for letting me know about the car," she said with false cheeriness. "And good luck at your meeting."

To his amazement, she began to close the door. "Hey, hold on." He reached out to stop her.

She looked at him questioningly.

"If you still want to come with me, you can," he blurted out.

"Really?" She stared at him as if she wasn't sure she'd heard right. Not that he blamed her. He was having a hard time believing it himself.

"Yeah." He ignored the little voice in his head demanding to know what in the hell he was doing.

She brightened. "I—I'd like that."

"You'll probably be bored," he warned.

"Oh, no. I'm sure it'll be interesting." She touched her fingertips self-consciously to the tender skin beneath her eyes. "Just let me wash my face and grab my purse."

"No rush. Take your time. I'll go pull the truck around."

"Okay."

He turned away, suddenly desperate to escape.

"Sterling?"

She laid her hand on his forearm and he jerked around, frustratingly aware of the burst of awareness her touch was causing him. "What?"

"Thanks." When she smiled this time, her face had a real glow of happiness.

"No problem." He gave her a nod, then hightailed it

for the stairs, asking himself again what the hell had just happened.

But no matter what kind of spin he tried to put on it, the answer came back the same. Although he could hardly believe it, it seemed he'd just asked Susan to go along on an appointment he didn't have.

Five

"I know it's none of my business," Susan said as she and Sterling drove away from McKisky's Wholesale Feed, their latest stop of the morning, "but is there something wrong with Mrs. McKisky?"

Sterling shot her a quick, guarded look. "Like what?"

She considered her answer. "I don't know exactly. She just seemed so surprised to see you. And then, when you gave her that huge order for feed...it was as if she couldn't decide whether to be shocked or pleased."

"Huh," he said neutrally, carefully checking the non-existent traffic before swinging the big pickup truck into the oncoming lane to avoid a tumbleweed that had blown onto the road. "She seemed okay to me."

Susan studied him from under her lashes. Although she was enjoying their outing, she had to admit they hadn't spent the morning even close to how she'd expected. Given Sterling's initial reluctance to have her accompany him, she'd just assumed his plans for the day included meeting with high-powered associates or scouting out some business he wanted to acquire or something else equally important and millionairelike.

Instead they'd spent their time running errands. They'd gone by the bank to cash a check. They'd dropped in at the hardware store—she still wasn't sure why, since they hadn't purchased anything—then stopped by the saddle-makers, where Sterling had been informed the bridle he'd ordered had been delivered to the house several weeks ago. Next, they'd driven to Crane to look at a Black Angus bull, then made their way to the feed brokers.

And though everyone at all those places had been pleased to see Sterling, they'd also seemed surprised at his presence. Susan hated to jump to conclusions, but she had the distinct impression that most, if not all, of their stops this morning had been spur-of-the-moment. As opposed to say...planned.

Not that she was complaining. At least they were together. And Sterling did seem to be trying. Though she'd hardly characterize him as chatty, the past few hours had been informative. She now knew he drank his coffee black, liked to drive fast and had a surprising weakness for jazz. She'd learned that he'd worked most of his life, starting with odd jobs in grade school, and that for all his success he didn't seem to care a whole lot about money. She knew he preferred to read history and other nonfiction, that he was a huge Dallas Cowboys fan and that he'd never wanted to live anywhere but West Texas.

Unfortunately she'd also found that every time they began to grow at ease with each other, he promptly withdrew. She couldn't imagine why, but it was almost as if he didn't want to like her.

She, on the other hand, clearly liked him too much. Despite her vow to act like a grown-up, such simple things as the brush of his hand or the way he drawled certain words continued to make her heart beat faster.

She couldn't seem to quell her awareness of him, either. Glancing over now, she found herself admiring the clean line of his profile, the muscular shape of his arms, the no-nonsense grip of his hands on the steering wheel. And remembering what it had been like on their wedding day when she'd been wrapped in those arms, touched by those hands and claimed by those warm, firm, masculine lips—

"That air conditioner too cold for you?"

She jumped, jarred out of her reverie. Meeting Sterling's gaze, she prayed he hadn't caught her staring again. "What? No. Not at all."

"You sure?"

"Yes. Why do you ask?"

He glanced over at her, his eyes shaded by the brim of his hat. He shrugged one broad shoulder. "You've got goose bumps."

"Oh." She glanced down. Sure enough, her arms had a light sprinkling of raised flesh. But that wasn't what brought the rush of heat to her cheeks. That was prompted by the sight of her tightly beaded nipples poking blatantly at the fabric of her shirt. And her guilty knowledge that the cause didn't have a thing to do with the air-conditioning. "You're right. Maybe it is a little chilly in here," she said, hastily crossing her arms.

"So why didn't you say so?" Lips tight, he reached out and adjusted the main vent, flipping it away from her and pointing it straight at him. He turned the fan to high.

Wondering what his problem was—she, after all, was

the one who'd just embarrassed herself—she faced forward and gazed out the windshield, feigning absorption in the scenery. "Where are we going now?"

"I need to drop by one of my ranches. I promised the man who runs it for me I'd drop off a computer inventory program he wants to try."

"Oh."

They passed a dusty grove of poplar trees and he turned onto a narrow dirt driveway. Squinting against the sun as the truck rattled over a cattle guard, she could see a small, tidy ranch house up ahead, flanked by a windmill, barn, several sheds and a maze of animal pens. Although the operation was modest, it looked prosperous and was as neat as a pin.

"This will only take a minute." Sterling slowed the truck and turned into a graveled parking area behind the house. "Then we'll go get some lunch."

"Okay."

Across the yard, the screen door on the house flew open and a little girl emerged. To Susan's amazement, the child leaped off the porch and came tearing toward them, waving her arms exuberantly. "Mr. Church! Hey, Mr. Church!"

Biting off a curse, Sterling swerved away from the small figure and hit the brakes. Slamming the transmission into Park, he rolled down the electric window as the pickup rocked to a halt and stuck his head out. "Clarissa Jane! What in Sam Hill are you trying to do? Get yourself run over?"

"Gee, Mr. Church," the child scoffed cheerfully, clambering onto the running board and hooking one small, tanned arm around the side mirror for security. "You'd never run over me. You're way too good a driver.'' Her heart-shaped face angelic, she beamed adoringly at him.

To Susan's amazement, it had the desired effect. Although she couldn't see all of Sterling's face, she could hear the softening in his voice as he said, ''I am, huh?''

''Yep.'' The little girl, who looked to be seven or eight, nodded enthusiastically, then craned her neck to stare at Susan with blatant curiosity. ''Who's that?''

He hesitated only the barest instant. ''That's my wife.''

''Really?''

''Really.'' He turned. ''Susan, this is Clarissa Moran,'' he explained. ''Her dad, Frank, runs the ranch.''

Susan smiled at the child. ''Hello, Clarissa.''

The little girl smiled back. ''Hi. You can call me Clarry. Everybody does, except when they're mad at me.'' She made a comical face, then shifted her gaze back to Sterling.

''Your mom and dad around?'' he inquired.

''Yep. Only Mama's taking a nap 'cuz she was up all night with the baby, and Daddy went to check on the cattle out by Arroyo Basin.''

''Ah. Well, you think you could run a package into the house for me?''

''Sure. But first—'' her eyes gleamed with suppressed anticipation ''—you gotta come out to the barn.''

''And why do I have to do that?''

The little girl's air of excitement grew. '''Cuz there's something I want to show you. You're gonna be *sooo* surprised.'' Wriggling with ill-suppressed glee, she glanced at Susan and added generously, ''She can come, too.''

"Hmm." He studied her elfin face for a moment, then he, too, glanced at Susan. "That okay with you?"

She smiled. "It's fine." At this point, wild horses couldn't have kept her away from that barn and the chance to observe Sterling with his unexpected friend.

"Okay then."

Without further ado, he released his seat belt and reached for the door handle. Susan followed suit. Walking around the front of the truck, she had to struggle to keep the surprise off her face as Clarry claimed Sterling's hand. Clasping it in her own, the child led the way across the hot, hard-packed ground toward the barn, chatting about recent events on the ranch with every step while Sterling steadfastly avoided Susan's gaze.

They entered the cavernous structure through a side door. Susan blinked for a moment as she waited for her eyes to adjust, then walked after the other two as they made for the far corner.

"Look, Mr. Church!" the child exclaimed, sinking down on her knees next to a shaggy black-and-white dog lying on a bed of straw. "Lucy had babies! Aren't they cool?"

"They sure are, honey," Sterling said, as a dozen fuzzy-faced puppies lurched unsteadily to their feet and crowded around him and the child. There was a husky note in his voice that Susan had never heard before.

"They're all spoken for, 'cuz everybody knows what a good dog Lucy is. Except for this one." Clarry scooped up a big-eyed pup with a black tail and black ears, and a mask of brown across its eyes. "She's the smartest and the cutest," she explained, "and I wouldn't let anybody take her." Climbing to her feet, she nuzzled her face against the soft little creature's, then straightened and solemnly thrust the puppy into Sterling's arms. "That's 'cuz I want *you* to have her, Mr. Church."

Unable to hide his surprise, Sterling clutched the squirming puppy, automatically cradling it in the crook of his arm. "You do?"

"Uh-huh. It's a present," Clarry confided happily. "From me to you. 'Cuz you gave Daddy your ranch to take care of when nobody else would and now we don't have to live with icky old Aunt Elizabeth anymore."

Sterling glanced down at the pup, then back at the child, and cleared his throat. "Gee, that's awful sweet of you, honey. And you're right about this little girl. She's pretty special."

The child's smile was radiant. "I knew you'd like her."

"I do." As if unable to help himself, he stroked his thumb over the puppy's bumpy spine, rewarded as the little creature snuggled closer, staring up at him with big, soft eyes. Yet when he finally glanced at Clarry, his face was sober. "And I really appreciate you wanting to give her to me. But the thing is—" regret seemed to weigh at his shoulders "—I can't take her."

Clarry's face fell. "Why not?"

"Because, honey, puppies need a lot of attention. Right now, I'm pretty busy, and it wouldn't be fair to take her just to stick her away in a kennel somewhere."

"But I want you to have her!"

He sighed. "I know, honey, but—"

"I could take care of her," Susan said quietly.

Instantly two sets of eyes turned to stare at her.

"Really?" Clarry was as easy to read as a large print book, going from crestfallen to hopeful in a split second.

Sterling's reaction was tougher to gauge. "You don't have to do that."

Susan bit her lip. There wasn't so much as a hint in his silvery-gray eyes that she'd done the right thing and she wondered if she'd totally misread him. "It's up to you, of course," she said, backpedaling madly. "I mean, I think it would be nice to have a dog, but I don't have any experience raising one. And I couldn't do it for another few weeks, not until they find a replacement for me at work..."

"But that's perfect!" Clarry declared. "The puppies aren't ready to leave Lucy yet anyway."

Sterling's gaze remained locked on Susan. "It'd be a lot of work. Are you sure?"

She glanced at the puppy resting against him, contentedly chewing on one of his shirt buttons while he absently stroked it with his fingertips, and all of a sudden she had her answer. "Yes," she said firmly. "Yes, I am." He might not be willing to admit it, but he needed that puppy. She just knew it.

He was silent another moment. Finally, however, he nodded. "Okay. I guess that means we've got us a dog."

Clarry whooped with happiness. "All right! Thanks, Mrs. Church!"

But it was Sterling's reaction that went straight to Susan's heart. He hesitated, then slowly offered the puppy to her. "Yeah. Thanks."

She smiled, her hands brushing his as she gathered the warm little bundle against her. "You're welcome."

For a second his expression didn't change. Then, almost reluctantly, he smiled back.

"You sure this is all right?" Sterling said gruffly, holding the door for Susan and motioning her to precede him into the Royal Diner.

She glanced at him over her shoulder. "It's fine. One

of my co-workers comes here all the time. She swears they have the best cheeseburgers in town."

"Huh," he said neutrally, wondering why she had to be so nice.

She smiled. "Besides, I don't think I could have walked a step farther."

He looked down at the buckskin cowboy boots gracing her feet and frowned. "Look, if those boots are hurting you, we can take them back—"

"They feel great, Sterling. Honest. I was referring to my stomach. The truth is, I'm starved, so it's a good thing this place is as close to the bootery as it is."

"Yeah, I suppose." He told himself there was no reason to feel guilty. After all, it wasn't as if he'd *planned* this. He'd merely wanted to get her some decent footwear after she'd nearly stepped on a nail in her flimsy tennis shoes out at Moran's. It was sheer coincidence that the boot shop happened to be kitty-corner from this particular café, the very one where Princess Anna was working.

Yet as long as he was here, he felt he had an obligation to check things out. The fact that it provided a welcome distraction from Susan was just icing on the cake.

The door swung shut behind him. He took a look around, confirming his first impression that the diner was simply your basic small-town café. A long counter with padded stools fronted the kitchen, a double row of tables occupied the center of the room and booths lined the rest of the walls. There was a revolving pie case next to the cash register and a lighted jukebox in one corner.

By far the best looking thing in the room was the elegant blonde serving pie to a couple of cowboys at the counter. She glanced over, doing a quick double take when she saw him. She was quick to recover, however, and promptly sent him a reserved smile. "Hello. If you'd like to take a seat, I'll be with you shortly."

"Thanks." He looked at Susan. "You care where we sit?"

"No. You go ahead and choose. I think I'll make a trip to the ladies' room."

Damned if his luck wasn't changing. He hadn't expected any time alone, but he wasn't complaining. "Okay."

"I'll see you in a minute."

He watched her walk away, his mouth twisting caustically as he realized that, improving luck or not, the seductive sway the boots added to her gait was having a predictable effect on his body.

Impatient with himself—he really had to get a grip—he wheeled and walked briskly to an empty booth along the least occupied section of wall in the diner. Yanking off his Stetson, he tossed it onto the seat, then sat down on the padded vinyl and concentrated on composing himself.

His "waitress" arrived a few minutes later. Handing him a pair of menus embossed with the logo The Royal Diner—Food Fit For A King!, she indicated the mug upside down on a paper coaster. "Coffee?"

"Please." He turned the cup upright, waiting until she leaned closer to add in an undertone, "It's nice to see you, Princess."

"And you, Mr. Churchill."

"Everything okay?"

"I'm doing very well, thank you."

"And Will?" In their short time together, Sterling had developed a real fondness for the princess's quiet young son.

"William is fine, too." She filled his cup, the heavy pot wobbling slightly in her hand. "This week he rather thinks he would like to become a Texas Ranger."

Sterling couldn't help it, he smiled. "That's good. Is there anything you two need? Anything I can do to make your stay more comfortable?"

"We're fine, really. Gregory has seen to everything." Not for the first time, he wondered at the undertone he could hear in her voice whenever she said Greg's name. Yet there was no time to dwell on it as she leaned closer and said, "Have you, perhaps, had any word about my precious little Edward and Miranda?"

He shook his head. "It's still too soon, Princess. Like we discussed, getting your niece and nephew out of Asterland is going to take considerably more time than your own liberation did. But don't worry—they'll be fine. Blake Hunt knows what he's doing."

"Of course," she said with a sudden touch of formality. "I didn't mean to imply that I don't trust him. He is Gregory's brother, after all."

"That's right, he is." For her sake, Sterling was careful not to let his own reservations show. While he'd trust Greg with his life—and had—Blake was another matter. Oh, there was no question about the younger Hunt brother's integrity or his ability to handle himself. But taking care of two small babies was a horse of a different color. Not that Sterling had any intention of telling the princess that. He was damned if he'd add to her worry.

Besides, it appeared they were out of time. Looking over, he saw Susan making her way across the room toward them. Careful to keep his movements casual, he sat back and reached for his cup. "Thanks for the coffee, miss," he said politely, taking a sip.

The princess was a quick study. Taking his cue, she

took a step back and graciously inclined her head. "You're welcome." She waited as Susan arrived and got seated, then inquired, "Would you care for some coffee?"

"No, thank you."

"Very well. I'm afraid my shift is over, but someone will be back in a few minutes to take your order." With a regal nod, she departed.

A faint frown marring her brow, Susan glanced after her.

"Something the matter?" Sterling asked.

She shifted her gaze, regarding him thoughtfully. "No. It's just, I thought— Is she a friend of yours?"

He tensed. Although his gut told him she could be trusted, the princess's secret was not his to share. He opened his mouth to say no, only to pause as he recalled her perceptiveness about Mrs. McKisky. "An acquaintance," he improvised. "She used to live in Midland. Why?"

Looking down, she smoothed her hand over the menu, answering with a question of her own. "Remember that first day, at my house, when you asked if I had someone I cared about?"

"Vaguely."

She looked up, her brown eyes suddenly troubled. "It just occurred to me that perhaps I should have asked you the same thing."

It took a second for her meaning to penetrate. When it did, he couldn't decide what was more troubling: the pang of gratification he felt that she cared how he felt, the immediate impulse he had to assure her there was nobody else—or the realization that she'd just innocently handed him the perfect way to regain some distance.

Because the more time he had to think about it, the

more he realized she was right. In order to raise a child together, they did need to achieve a certain degree of camaraderie. What's more, there was too much at stake to risk screwing it up by rushing things.

The kicker was, he was in danger of doing just that thanks to the downright overpowering physical attraction he felt for her.

And Susan definitely wasn't helping any. It was bad enough she was so pretty. But her offer to take Clarry's puppy had also made it clear she had a kind heart and the courage to act on her instincts. Added to that, she was also darn good company. Bottom line, he'd enjoyed himself today—except for those instances when he'd caught her staring at him like a schoolgirl who'd just discovered her sexuality. Then she'd about driven him crazy.

Even so, he didn't doubt for an instant that if he told her there'd been somebody else, she'd back off in an instant and give him some space to get over his "loss."

Yet as their gazes meshed, he knew he wasn't going to do it. No matter how imperative he felt it was to take things slow and easy, he simply couldn't take advantage of her good nature that way. And though he'd no doubt regret it later—hell, who was he kidding? He was regretting it already—he didn't want to start off their marriage with that kind of lie. He'd just have to suck it in, act like a man and find the strength to do the right thing. And he'd better start now, before he changed his mind.

"If you're asking me if I had to break off with someone to marry you, the answer is no," he said, getting it over with.

"Oh." She hesitated a second, then smiled, looking relieved. "I guess it's not very noble of me, but I'm glad. This whole situation is hard enough as it is."

The understatement of the century. He took a sip of coffee, more than ready to change the subject. "You given any thought to a name for the puppy?"

"Heavens, no. I was hoping you'd have some ideas."

"You were?"

"Yes."

He told himself it was childish to be pleased, but he was anyway. "I'll think about it." A new thought struck him. "What about the baby?"

"What about it?"

"You have any names picked out?"

Her expression suddenly turned shy. "Actually I did sort of think that if it's a girl, I'd like to call her Maggie, after my mom. But then, that was before you and I got together. I certainly wouldn't want to slight your mother or make her feel left out."

"Trust me, you don't want to name the baby after my mother," he said flatly.

Her eyes widened a little. Yet with the sensitivity he was beginning to realize was an integral part of her nature, she didn't press. "All right."

"It's just not the sort of thing she cares about," he went on, not sure why he felt compelled to say more. "Maggie is fine."

She nodded. "Okay."

"Good. That's settled." They'd worry about a name for a boy later, he thought, relieved as another waitress came bustling up.

Plucking a pencil from above her ear, the woman, a stout brunette in her fifties, flipped open her order book and scowled at them. "You folks know what you want?"

Sterling raised an eyebrow at Susan in question.

"I'm sorry," she said, looking from him to the waitress. "I haven't had a chance to look at the menu yet. It'll only take me a second to decide, though, and in the meantime I'd really appreciate a glass of ice water—"

"Fine," the woman snapped. She rammed the pencil back into her hair, shoved the order pad back in her pocket and glared belligerently at Sterling. "What about you? You want water, too?"

He stiffened, not much liking her attitude. "No. More coffee, please."

"Figures." She spun on her heel and stomped over to the busing station, where she noisily scooped ice into a glass, added water, then snatched up the coffeepot and marched back. She slapped down the glass and filled his coffee cup to the brim in a trice. Then, smacking the pot down on the tabletop, she retrieved pencil and pad and stared impatiently at them. "Well?"

Sterling had about had enough. "Susan?" he said quietly.

"I'll have the turkey sandwich, with some fruit and a glass of milk."

"You want that on white or wheat?"

"White."

"Humph," the waitress muttered disapprovingly before turning her beady eyes on Sterling.

He met her disagreeable gaze with a steely one of his own. "I'd like the chicken-fried steak," he said in a tone that dared her to comment.

Not about to be cowed, she reached out and snatched up the menus. "Whatever." With that, she grabbed the coffeepot and stormed toward the kitchen, ignoring several other customers' frantic signals for service.

Sterling couldn't believe it. Holding onto his temper by a thread, he glanced at Susan, who was watching the

waitress's progress across the room with obvious aston-
ishment.

As if she felt his gaze, she looked his way. "Oh, my."
Her lips twitched with amusement. "I hope she isn't
expecting a tip."

He stared at her, incredulous.

She glanced down at the table. "Sorry." She swallowed and looked back up. "But if you could just see
your face—" She clapped a hand to her mouth to
smother a giggle.

Damned if that muted sound wasn't contagious.
Against his will, Sterling felt the corners of his own
mouth quiver as the absurdity of the encounter caught
up with him. He sat there a long moment, listening to
her struggle for control. Just as she seemed to get it, he
said solemnly, "Susan?"

"Hmm?"

"Just for the record...my mother's name is Hor-
tense."

"It is?"

He nodded. "And her middle name is Hedwig."

"Oh, dear."

He made a face. "Yeah."

It was too much for her. She lost it, albeit demurely.

With a rusty chuckle, Sterling joined in, unable to
remember the last time he'd laughed.

Yet underlying his mirth, he felt a sort of good-
natured despair. Because for the umpteenth time that
day, his whole body felt hot and tight.

When it came to Susan, it seemed even laughter was
an aphrodisiac.

Six

Susan slicked back her wet hair as she climbed from the pool. Although she'd swum only a half-dozen laps, it still felt good to get some exercise. With a contented sigh, she picked up the oversize beach towel she'd left on the deck, dried herself off, then padded over and settled into one of the half-dozen chaises that faced the water.

There was something deliciously decadent about having an entire pool all to yourself, she thought as she closed her eyes and tipped her face toward the sun. Just as there was something wonderfully lazy about lying around at ten on a Saturday morning. She wouldn't want to do it every day, of course—she firmly believed that everyone needed responsibilities and a purpose in life— but at the moment it sure felt nice.

Particularly since she wasn't sleeping very well at night.

She made a face, acknowledging that her insomnia didn't make a whole lot of sense. Thanks to the switch from full- to part-time at work, and the luxury of getting to drive to the library in air-conditioned comfort instead of having to get there under her own power, she was feeling a lot better lately. Adding to her sense of well-being, Maxine was seeing to it that she was eating better, too.

As for Sterling, the past week had seen a steady improvement in their relationship. She wasn't sure what had made the difference, whether it was her offer to take on the puppy, that moment of shared laughter at the diner, or simply her original appeal to his reason, but he was no longer avoiding her. On the contrary, he was making a real effort to include her in his daily life, while treating her with all the courtesy and respect that befitted the mother of his child.

Not that he'd done a complete about-face. At times he still tended to be prickly. And cool, contained, remote and reserved if it suited him. And he was never going to win any prizes for being an easy conversationalist.

Yet for all of that, it hadn't taken her long to realize he was the kind of man you could depend on. And though he downplayed his many kindnesses, beneath his tough facade he clearly cared about doing right by others, whether it was something as minor as buying boots for his new wife's feet or something as major as protecting a little girl's feelings.

Then again, he didn't make such insights easy; despite their burgeoning friendship, Sterling continued to maintain a wall of reserve Susan couldn't get past. It was especially true of his past, particularly when it came to his mother and his first marriage. But it also applied more broadly to the present. She hadn't missed the way he'd tensed when she'd asked him about that striking blond waitress at the Royal Diner. And though she didn't doubt he'd told her the truth since there was no reason not to, it was just further proof that he wasn't a man given to easy confidences.

Even so, she liked him. And when she thought about it rationally, she knew she should be sleeping like a log.

But she wasn't. Instead she was starting to dread bedtime, since it seemed all she did was toss and turn for hours, plagued by a vague longing for something she couldn't identify.

Oh, she knew what part of the problem was—she wasn't *that* naive. She was physically attracted to Sterling, and had been from the day they met. Whether it was a matter of chemistry, or simply some strange twist of her pregnancy, she found him incredibly exciting. She wanted to experience his touch and touch him back and do all sorts of daring, delicious, scandalous things. And the more she tried to block that heated need from her mind, the harder it got not to think about it all the time.

Yet there was also something more. A longing that was even stronger, deeper, more compelling than just sex...

Suddenly she felt exhausted. Typical of her pregnancy, tiredness seemed to roll over her like an incoming tide, making it impossible to think. Yawning, she settled more comfortably into the chaise, knowing that it wouldn't do any good to fight it. She'd just rest for a minute...

She must have drifted off. Because the next time she opened her eyes, she was no longer alone. Sterling was standing on the opposite end of the yard, inside the fence, grooming one of the horses. Blinking the sleep from her eyes, she realized he appeared more relaxed than she'd ever seen him.

She sat up. And though the old Susan, the shy, un-assertive one, urged her to stay put, the new, adventurous Susan insisted it would be rude not to say hi, and it wasn't long before she'd climbed to her feet. Drawing on the short cotton shirt that served as her swimsuit cover, she crossed the pool deck, went up the steps and across the flagstone terrace to the lawn.

She stopped a few feet short of the fence, the cool grass tickling her bare feet. But before she could say a word, Sterling abruptly turned, as if he'd sensed her presence. For one long moment as his gaze swept over her he seemed gripped by an indefinable tension, but it disappeared so quickly she was sure she'd imagined it.

"Hi," she said lightly.

"'Morning. Been for swim?"

"Yes. I thought I'd do it before it got too hot."

He twisted back around and resumed brushing the horse's shiny brown coat. "Good idea."

Her stomach hollowed as she watched his broad shoulders flex under his old black T-shirt. "You're certainly hard at work."

He shrugged. "I guess."

She swallowed. "Do you do this kind of chore often?"

He ducked under the rope anchoring the horse to the fence and began brushing its other side, starting at the neck and working his way back. "Depends."

"On what?"

He glanced at her over the horse's back, his gaze touching briefly on her bare legs before he brought his eyes to her face. "My schedule. The weather. Different things."

"I thought Kenny and Ernesto took care of the horses." The two men were part of a small army of people Sterling employed to take care of various things on the estate.

"They do. But I like to keep my hand in."

"I see." And she did. The more she got to know him, the more she realized that he had a highly developed sense of responsibility.

As if to prove her point, his gaze flicked over her again and he frowned. "You'd better be careful or you'll get sunburned." He ran the brush over the horse's rump and down its haunch. "It may be almost October but the sun's still plenty hot."

"Don't worry," she replied, warmed by his concern. "I never go out without sunscreen. Although—" she examined her arm, pleased to see a faint blush of color instead of her usual milky paleness "—it does look like I've managed to get a little bit of a tan."

"Well, don't get too much." Stepping away from the horse, he moved up to the fence, gesturing her closer. "Can you put this in the carry-all—" he handed her the brush and indicated a yellow plastic container near her feet "—and get me the hoof pick? That's it on the bottom, that metal hook with the red handle."

"Sure." Happy to oblige, she set down the brush, found the desired tool and cautiously moved forward to hand it to him, only to gasp as the horse he'd been brushing abruptly stretched out its neck and thrust its nose at her. "Oh!" Startled, she scrambled backward, the hoof pick dropping from her nerveless fingers.

"Susan? What's wrong?" Sending her a puzzled glance, Sterling bent down to retrieve the pick.

"Nothing. That is—I—it— Oh!" She watched in

alarm as another horse, this one an enormous gray, came up behind him. "Watch out!"

He straightened, calmly pushing the animal away. "Relax. It's just Rockaway." He gave the gray an affectionate slap on the shoulder. "He wouldn't hurt a mouse. Neither would Cassie here." He indicated the horse he'd been brushing. "She probably thought you had a treat for her or something."

"Oh." She let out her breath, feeling foolish. "Sorry. I guess I overreacted."

"Yeah, I guess so." He considered her a moment, totally at ease as the gray rubbed its head against his shoulder. "You have a bad experience with a horse or something?"

She shook her head. "No. They're just so big. I guess they make me a little nervous." She smiled apologetically. "There aren't a lot of horses in libraries."

"I suppose not."

She sighed, wishing she were braver. "I guess now that I live someplace where they're everywhere, I need to learn to relax, don't I?"

"It couldn't hurt."

She nodded. "You're right. After all, our baby deserves better than a 'fraidy-cat for a mother."

"Well, yeah, I guess."

She recalled how content he'd looked earlier, before she'd interrupted. As much as she'd like to ask for his help, she hated to intrude on even more of his private time. "I suppose I could check out some books on horses when I go into work today," she said, thinking out loud. "Then later, if it's okay with you, I could ask Ernesto to let me help out at the stables until I feel more comfortable."

Maybe it was her imagination, but he seemed to

stiffen. "You don't have to do that. I can show you whatever you need to know."

"That's really nice of you, Sterling, but I don't want to bother you."

"Fine. I guess I can't blame you if you'd rather learn from Ernesto."

Oh, dear. She *had* hurt his feelings. Instantly contrite, she said hastily, "Oh, it's not that—"

"Good. Because I don't want you working in the stable, wearing yourself out. Not in your condition."

To her shock, she felt an undeniable burst of irritation. She knew he was merely trying to be nice, but it stung nonetheless that he was only making the offer because she was pregnant, not because he wanted to be with her for herself.

Except that he was under no obligation to feel that way, she reminded herself sharply, ashamed of her uncharitable thoughts. And he had every right to be concerned about their child. "You're right," she said quietly.

"Then it's settled. We'll start this afternoon." Shooing away the affectionate Rockaway, he turned his back to her, leaned against the bay's shoulder and gave the animal some sort of mysterious signal that caused it to raise its foot.

Susan stared at his backside. She knew she ought to count her blessings and be glad that he so obviously cared about the baby. Yet as the breeze came up and ruffled his dark hair, making her suddenly yearn to touch him herself, she found herself thinking it wasn't enough.

Not by a long shot.

"So where'd this little fellow come from?" Sterling asked his friend Becky Sullivan as he unlatched the back of her ancient horse trailer.

She tucked a loose strand of bright red hair behind her ear. Swinging open the trailer doors, she stepped up into the dim interior with the easy confidence of someone who'd spent her whole life around livestock. "I got a call a few weeks ago from an elderly lady with a few acres up near Big Spring," she said over her shoulder. "Lou Verstadt—" she named a local veterinarian "—gave her my name because you were out of town. She'd sold her place and was going to live with her daughter in Austin, and she couldn't stand the thought of having Shorty here put down."

"Huh." He stepped to one side, getting out of the way as Becky competently backed a compact pinto pony out into the yard in front of his stable.

"I can't say that I blame her." She stood still a moment, letting the animal, which was brown and white and had bright little eyes and a comically bushy mane and tail, get his land legs. "I've had him over at my place the past few days, and he's a character. Twice he's unlatched the corral gate, moseyed on up to the house and stood by the back door as if he expected to be let in." Her green eyes softened beneath the brim of her hat. "Truth to tell, he's so cute I almost let him."

"Oh, that's just what you need," Sterling chided, knowing she already had more horses than she could easily handle. "You'll both be better off with him here. What did you say his name was?" Leading the way, he walked into the stable and toward one of the roomy box stalls with the attached corral that would be the newcomer's home for the next few days.

"It's Shortcake. Shorty for short. I've got his paperwork out in the truck." She led the pony into the stall, unclipped the lead line and joined Sterling in the corridor, watching as he shut the lower half of the double door and secured the latch. With the ease of the old friends they were, the two of them stood in relaxed silence, observing the diminutive pinto as it checked out its new surroundings.

Sterling supposed that to some people their friendship might seem odd, given Becky's modest means and his own current wealth. Yet they had a lot in common. Not only did they both love horses, but they'd each grown up knowing a degree of financial hardship—and what it was to deal with a difficult parent. And since they were both prone to keeping their stronger emotions to themselves, they also tended to respect each other's privacy. Introduced right after Sterling's divorce by a mutual friend at a local horse auction, they'd been surprised to find they were extremely comfortable with each other, and their friendship had proceeded from there.

"So." Becky turned, propped her shoulder negligently against the wall and crossed her arms. "I read the most interesting thing in this morning's paper. Right there in the 'What's Happening in Royal' column was this item stating that Mr. Sterling Churchill, CEO of Churchill Enterprises, had recently married Miss Susan Wilkins in a private ceremony at the city courthouse." She paused, giving him a pointed look. "'Course I didn't believe it. There's no way my good friend Sterling would get married and forget to tell me about it. Particularly when the last I heard he wasn't even dating."

Sterling tried to look contrite. "I guess I should've called you, huh?"

She rolled her eyes. "Now there's an idea." Sobering, she looked consideringly at him. "Then it's true? The guy at the paper didn't just make it up? You're really married?''

''Yeah.''

''To that little auburn-haired gal who works at the library?''

''One and the same.''

She shook her head, clearly bemused. ''I don't believe it. I thought you were never getting hitched again. What happened?''

He shoved a hand through his hair, uncharacteristically tempted to share the whole story. It would be a relief to tell someone how something that sounded comical—a snafu at the Buddy Clinic—had turned his whole life on its ear. Not to mention how Susan had gone from frumpy to fabulous overnight, how his hormones seemed to be in a permanent state of overdrive and how lately he didn't seem to know if he were coming or going.

Take that lunacy yesterday, when Susan had admitted that horses made her nervous. If he'd had the sense God gave a jackrabbit, he would have kept his mouth shut when she'd suggested going to Ernesto for help.

But had he? Shoot, no. He'd been so busy trying not to stare at all the gentle curves revealed by her swimsuit, he'd simply reacted, instantly rejecting the thought of her doing *anything* with another man. As a consequence, he'd spent two agonizing hours with her here in the stable yesterday afternoon, watching her get more and more relaxed with the horses while he'd grown more and more uptight with *her*. Worse, he'd promised to put himself through another session of hands-off torture a little later today.

None of which he had any intention of telling Becky, he abruptly realized. For one thing, it was far too personal. For another, it would be wrong to talk to someone

else about things he had no intention of discussing with
Susan. She was his wife, and whatever was—or was
not—between them was private, not for public con-
sumption. Royal was a small town. The fewer people
who knew the details of his marriage and his child's
conception, the better.

Besides, confidences weren't his style, which Becky
knew damn well. "Everything just happened real fast,"
he said carefully. "I met Susan, we talked, we decided
to get married." Well, hell. It was sort of the truth.

"Just like that?"

"Just like that."

There was a lengthy silence. He braced, certain that
Becky was going to see right through him when suddenly she sighed, taking him totally by surprise. "How
romantic." She paused, then shocked him a second time
as she blurted out, "I wish something like that would
happen to me."

"You do?"

"Yeah. I'd love to be swept off my feet." Her expression turned rueful and she sighed again. "Not that
it's ever going to happen. Heck, probably the only way
I'm ever going to get married is if I hold Woody to the
promise he made me when I was eighteen."

Sterling frowned, hearing an unexpected touch of vul-
nerability beneath her breezy manner. "What's Forrest
got to do with this?" Forrest Cunningham, whom only
Becky was allowed to call "Woody," was a fellow
member of the Cattleman's Club, and had made the trip
with Sterling to bring Princess Anna out of Obersbourg.
The Cunningham family's highly successful cattle ranch
adjoined the Sullivan's much more modest operation,
and while Sterling knew that Becky and Forrest had

practically grown up together, he'd never heard of any romance between the two.

From her expression, it was clear Becky already regretted having said anything. "Nothing. Just forget it—"

"Not a chance," he interrupted, glad for a reason to focus on somebody else's life for a change.

She sent him a puzzled glance, clearly surprised by his unusual persistence. "All right. If you have to know, I was feeling down, certain I'd never have a date much less a husband, so Woody said that if I wasn't married by the time I was thirty, he'd marry me himself. Like I said, I was just a kid, and he was just being kind. I'd forgotten all about it, but my birthday's coming up and…" She shrugged. "When I saw that thing in the paper about you, it popped into my head."

There was something in her face that told Sterling there was more going on than she claimed. Yet under the circumstances, he felt he'd pressed all he had a right to.

"See, I told you it was nothing," Becky said yet again. "Besides, I'm holding out for the real thing. Which—" she narrowed her eyes at him "—brings us back to you."

"No," he said firmly, "it doesn't. I've said all I intend to."

She studied him. "Like that, is it?"

"That's right."

She pursed her lips thoughtfully, then abruptly smiled. "All right. So when do I get to meet the new Mrs. Churchill?"

"I don't know. Soon."

"Aren't you at least going to have a reception or something?"

He shrugged. "Maybe. I hadn't really thought about it."

"Well, you should."

"We'll see," he said in a tone that made it clear that he was done with the subject.

Becky was silent a moment. Then, with the easygoing manner that helped make their friendship possible, she touched her hand lightly to his shoulder. "Well, congratulations anyway. You deserve some happiness. Now, if you don't mind, let's go get that paperwork so I can get out of here. I need to get home and feed my stock."

Sterling nodded. Yet as he followed her out to her truck and waved her off, he found himself thinking that she wouldn't be so quick with her congratulations if she knew the truth.

Nor did his mood improve when he glanced at his watch and saw Susan was due to arrive any minute for Torture Session Number Two.

Sterling strode into the kitchen, his boot heels clicking loudly on the immaculate tile floor.

"Hey, boss." Maxine looked up from the pot she was stirring. "How you doin'?"

"Just great," he said sourly. He yanked off his hat and impatiently wiped the sweat from his brow with the back of his hand.

"I hope you're hungry, 'cuz I'm making my three-alarm chili for dinner and mmm-mmm, it's good."

"I'm sure it is. Have you seen, Susan? Is she upstairs?" Not waiting for an answer, he started in that direction.

"As a matter of fact, she's not."

He skidded to a stop. Wheeling around, he stared at his housekeeper, struggling to hold onto his temper.

"Then where is she? She was supposed to meet me down at the stable twenty minutes ago." He wasn't quite sure why he was so bent out of shape, but he was. For one thing, he didn't like being stood up. And the fact that he'd been stood up for something he didn't particularly want to do in the first place only seemed to make it worse.

Maxine reached for the pepper, calmly adding some to the mixture on the stove before she answered. "She must've forgotten. She came downstairs about four with a book, said she was in the mood for a walk, so she thought she'd hike down to the lake and read for a while."

Sterling frowned. "That was an hour and a half ago."

Maxine shrugged. "Maybe it's a real good book."

"Yeah. Or maybe something's wrong. Did you ever think of that?" He slapped his hat back on and headed for the door.

"Now, boss. Relax. You're overreacting. I'm sure she just lost track of the—"

The rest of her reassurance was lost in the smack of the door swinging shut behind him. Mouth set in a grim line, he walked directly across the yard and went over the fence, choosing to cut across the back pasture rather than walk around to the road.

With every step, he told himself he wasn't worried. Short of falling in the lake, or having a run-in with a snake, there really wasn't a whole lot that could happen to a person out here. Since Susan could swim, and snakes usually preferred laying out in the heat to hanging around the water, the odds were she was fine.

Of course, accidents did happen. People slipped and fell all the time for no discernible reason—people who weren't also pregnant. In addition, every once in a while a drifter turned up on the property, usually somebody down on their luck who'd walked in off the highway looking for a meal.

But he wasn't worried. Not really.

He vaulted the fence at the bottom of the pasture and headed for the grove of trees that curved around the far end of the lake. In a fit of industry last summer, he'd had the area nearest the water cleared, put in a picnic table and some chairs, as well as a rope swing and a hammock, thinking it would be a nice place to go on hot summer evenings. It was the obvious place for Susan to be.

He was glad for the wide path as he went from the bright sunshine into the mottled shade of the tree canopy. He slowed slightly as the path curved around an enormous oleander, then slowed even more as it skirted a tightly packed screen of cypress trees before taking a sharp bend and opening into the clearing. Which was a damn good thing, since as it was he nearly mowed Susan down as he came around the corner.

"Oh!" She stumbled back, her book slipping to the ground in the process.

He shot out his arms to steady her. "Easy."

"Sterling!" She looked up at him with a mixture of surprise and dawning pleasure. "What are you doing here?"

"Looking for you."

"Oh, dear." She made a face. "I'm late, I know. I'm sorry. I hope I didn't worry you."

He let go of her and took half a step back, the relief he'd been feeling abruptly displaced by annoyance at what seemed like a pretty glib apology to him. "No. Of course not."

"Oh, good—"

"Although I'd sure like to know why you didn't show up."

"Of course." She bit her lower lip, suddenly looking faintly embarrassed. "I'm afraid I fell asleep."

"What?"

"I laid down on the hammock to read, and I fell asleep."

He took a really good look at her, belatedly noticing that her blouse was wrinkled and her hair was tumbled around her face. Of more concern, as he studied her upturned face, he saw the faint shadows under her eyes. "You've been doing that a lot lately." Even to his own ears, it sounded like an accusation.

"Doing what?"

"Sleeping during the day. You were doing it out by the pool yesterday morning."

"Well, yes, but—"

"That does it, then." Swiveling around, he began to retrace his steps along the path.

She hurried after him. Reaching his side, she turned to stare at him, her dark eyes intent. "That does what?"

"That does it with your job."

Her shoulder bumped his as she struggled to keep up with his longer stride. "What does my job have to do with this?"

"Even working part-time is obviously too much for you. You'll just have to tell them you quit."

"What?" She stopped in surprise.

"You heard me." He kept walking.

"Sterling! That's ridiculous. My job has nothing to do with this." She launched herself after him.

"Right."

"It doesn't! And—and I don't have any intention of quitting. And would you please hold still for a moment?'' Instinctively she reached out and gripped his forearm.

He stopped and swung around to face her. He knew he was behaving badly, but he couldn't seem to help it. Somewhere along the line, he'd reached his limit. Still, he supposed he owed her the courtesy of hearing her out. ''Fine. If it's not your job, then what is it?''

''I'm just not sleeping well.''

''Because you're overtired.''

''Well, yes—''

''From working too hard.''

''Trust me, it's not that.''

''Then what is it, Susan?''

She stared up at him, her eyes locked on his. ''Oh, Sterling. Don't you know?''

''Obviously not.''

She squeezed her eyes shut for an instant. When she opened them, she seemed to have come to some sort of decision. ''It's this.'' To his shock, she slid her hands up his bare forearms, came up on tiptoe and pressed her lips to his.

Seven

She'd lost her mind, Susan thought wildly.

Any second now, Sterling was going to reach out and push her away. And when he did, she just knew she was going to die, done in by humiliation at his rejection.

Not that she could blame him. He couldn't be any more shocked than she was by her behavior. One moment she'd been standing there, a little overcome as she always was in his presence, wishing desperately that there was some rational way to tell him about her feelings. In the next, the little voice in her head had said, "Stop being such a coward. Isn't this supposed to be a whole new life? Aren't you done being the kind of woman who always fades into the woodwork? If you can't tell him how you feel, show him instead."

So she had.

And oh, it was wonderful. Everything about him felt right, from the hard, warm muscle of his arms against her palms, to the chiseled contours of his mouth against her lips. He smelled divine, too, the faint citrusy scent of his aftershave mixed with a musky hint of sweat.

If only he weren't so...rigid. It was as if her touch had turned him into a statue.

He was clearly still stunned. And though it probably wouldn't last much longer, she abruptly decided she might as well wrest every speck of pleasure from her reckless act that she could. As the old Texas saying went, if you were going to be hanged as a horse thief, you might as well take the whole herd as a single nag.

She threw caution to the winds. Sliding her hands up his rock-hard arms, she stepped closer, hardly able to believe her own boldness as she brushed up against his solid warmth. She twined her hands around his neck, tipped her head sideways and rubbed her lips against his, not caring when she dislodged his hat.

For a handful of seconds he continued to stand as stationary as a boulder. Then a low sound issued from deep in his throat. In the next instant his arms wrapped powerfully around her. He yanked her closer, pressing her into his hard contours. His lips parted beneath hers, and suddenly *he* was kissing *her* with an unrestrained hunger that would have frightened her had it been anyone else. But this was Sterling, and she trusted him...

He slid his hands under her T-shirt and rubbed the bare skin of her back. Pleasure ripped through her. It increased as he slanted his head and his tongue skated heatedly over her bottom lip.

She opened her mouth, unable to stop a faint moan as the kiss turned hot and carnal. Instinctively she recognized the suggestive rhythm he initiated and her knees went weak. She tightened her grip on his neck, but it was unnecessary as he pulled her even closer, crushing her aching breasts against his solid chest and pressing the cradle of her thighs against the hard ridge of his arousal.

For a second, she was so overwhelmed with sensation she was afraid she might faint. It suddenly seemed incredible that she could have reached the ripe old age of twenty-eight and never experienced this overwhelming desire. Or known that her whole body could ache with need for a man's touch. *Sterling's* touch.

She arched her back and tangled her fingers in the thick, silky hair at his nape, then slid her fingers under his collar. From the day they'd met, she'd wondered what it would be like to touch him. Now, she knew. His skin felt hot and smooth, like sun-warmed marble. She couldn't stop a groan of pleasure.

She felt Sterling shudder and lift his head. She opened her eyes. Only inches apart, they stared at each other. His eyes glittered, so dark they looked black, and she could feel the harsh wash of his breath against her damp, tender lips. With a sigh of mingled need and pleasure, she let her eyes drift shut and leaned forward, seeking his mouth once again.

Abruptly he stepped back, catching her by the shoulders as she swayed toward him. "Don't," he rasped.

Her eyes flew open. As she regained her balance, she tried to understand what the problem was. "Don't what?"

He let loose of her and took another step back, his chest heaving. Reaching up, he shoved his hands through his hair, then dropped his arms to his sides. "We shouldn't be doing this."

She fought to clear the sexual haze from her mind, to focus on what he was saying. "We shouldn't?"

"No."

"Why not?" Her stomach suddenly sank. "Is it me? Did I do something wrong?" She was pretty sure she knew the answer since she'd felt his arousal, but she still had to ask.

"Hell, no," he said harshly, his answer reassuringly immediate.

"Then what's the matter?"

He looked around, not saying anything immediately. Spotting his hat on the ground, he leaned over, dusted it off and settled it on his head. Not until his eyes were safely shaded did he turn to face her again. "It's too soon."

"Too soon for what?"

"For us to have sex."

Susan opened her mouth to protest, to point out that they'd only kissed, then shut it as she realized he was right. Given a little more time, that was exactly where things had been headed.

She wasn't sorry, either. All of a sudden, she felt as if she'd been waiting for him—and this—her whole life. If she had a regret, it was that they'd stopped.

It didn't take a Ph.D. to figure out that wasn't something she ought to share with Sterling right now, however. A glance at the tense set of his jaw was enough to tell her he felt strongly about whatever was bothering him. No matter how hard it was, some diplomacy was called for.

She conjured up a weak smile. "Well...at least we're married. That ought to count for something."

He shook his head, his expression grim. "No. That's just it. We're already going to be parents. We got married quickly. I don't think we should rush into anything else."

For the life of her, Susan didn't know what to say.

What he said made sense—in a way. Everything *had* happened fast. And in terms of actual time, they hadn't known each other that long.

And yet, he *was* her husband. And she didn't need any more time to know what kind of a man he was. What's more, she'd never, ever felt about anyone the way she did about him.

"We're both adults," she said softly. "If we both want the same thing, I don't see the harm—"

"It's too much, too soon," he insisted.

"But Sterling—"

"You're not thinking clearly, Susan."

"That's not true," she protested.

"Yes, it is." His expression closed, he started to turn away.

"But shouldn't we at least talk about this?"

"There's nothing to discuss," he said forcefully. "I'm heading back to the house. Are you coming?" Not waiting for her answer, he walked away, his long, booted legs churning up the terrain.

For the second time in two days, she found herself staring at his backside, her emotions in turmoil.

Only this time, she realized, following slowly after him, she finally knew what she wanted.

Sterling stared broodingly at the heavy cut-crystal glass in his hand.

He'd ordered the rare and expensive Scotch on the rocks forty-five minutes ago, taken one sip and had since spent his time watching the ice melt.

So what did that say about his character? That he was a bust as a sinner?

Big surprise.

He scowled, impatiently setting the glass down on the

table so hard that it sent diluted Scotch splashing onto his fingers. Leaning back in the oversize leather chair placed in the shadows of the room's far corner, he looked around the familiar interior of the Cattleman's Club cigar lounge, hoping for some sort of a diversion.

Unfortunately there was none to be found. As had been the case for the entire hour he'd been there, the place was about as lively as a crypt. The only signs of life came from the bartender and a pair of waiters, who were standing at the far end of the ornate bar, quietly going over next week's schedule.

It figured. Nothing had gone his way today.

Oh, yeah. There's nothing worse than finding out your wife wants to make love with you—

He bit off a curse and clamped down on his thoughts, determined not to go there. Reconsidering his drink, he picked it up and forced himself to take another sip, even though his heart wasn't in it. He'd given up hard drinking for good in his early twenties, after a binge with a bunch of Marine buddies. It had only taken that once for him to decide that no amount of temporary oblivion was worth the resulting loss of control. He really hated losing control....

"This a private party?"

He jerked his head up, surprised and pleased to see his friend Greg Hunt. "Hell, no. Have a seat." Grateful for the unexpected company, he waited for the other man to get settled and order a drink before stretching out his legs and asking, "What're you doing here? I thought you were supposed to be in court in Austin this week."

Greg shrugged. "I am. But there were some matters here at home that needed taking care of. I'm planning to fly over in the morning." He fell silent as the waiter delivered his drink. He took a sip, then looked curiously at Sterling. "Besides, you're one to talk. I read in the paper this morning that you got married."

That damn paper, Sterling thought blackly. He ought to buy the thing and shut it down for all the unwanted explanations it was causing him. "Yeah, I did."

"Well, that's great." Looking puzzled at Sterling's less-than-festive mood, he said mildly, "So what are you doing here? I'd think you'd be at home, tucked away with your new bride."

"I will be shortly," Sterling lied. "I had to run into town to get some papers from the office and decided to drop by and see if Hank was back from his honeymoon."

"I see." Greg took another sip of his drink. "I believe he's due back at the end of the week."

"Yeah. I know that now."

"I suppose he'll be living at his place in Pine Valley now that he's finally tied the knot."

"I'd imagine so."

"So what about you? You planning on making any major changes now that you're married?"

Sterling heard the curiosity in his friend's voice, but knew Greg was too well-mannered, and too private himself, to press the issue. Since he wasn't ready to reveal his impending fatherhood—the past few days had convinced him it would be best to let the interest in his marriage subside first—all he said was, "No. I don't think so."

"Pretty sudden, wasn't it?"

"Yeah, it was." Determined to change the subject once and for all, he said abruptly, "I stopped by the diner and checked on the princess last week."

Greg shifted in his chair. Maybe it was Sterling's

imagination, but his friend suddenly seemed to grow a little distant. "And?"

"She seemed to be doing all right."

"Good."

There was definitely an edge to the other man's voice. A month ago, Sterling would have pretended not to notice. But that was then, and this was now... He eyed his friend curiously. "So what's the story with you two?"

"What do you mean?"

"I mean there must be some sort of history between you. After all, she did call you when she needed to be rescued."

For a second he didn't think Greg was going to answer. Then the other man gave a slight shrug and said coolly, "We were briefly involved a few years ago when I was finishing up my stint with the military in Obersbourg. I didn't know she was a princess. When I found out...well, it was obvious that it wouldn't work. She had obligations to her country and to her family, just as she does now..." His voice trailed off as he lifted his glass to his lips and took a long swallow.

It was more than Sterling had expected him to say, and he decided not to press his luck. He nodded. "Yeah, I know what you mean. She is worried about her niece and nephew. And she's concerned that we hadn't heard anything from Blake. I told her it's still too soon, that everything would be fine, but I have to tell you, I've got some questions of my own."

"About what?"

"About Blake. I know he's done some hush-hush stuff for the government, and I'm not questioning his ability to pull this thing off, but once he does—what does he know about taking care of babies, anyway?"

"Relax," Greg said persuasively, his blue eyes intent.

"I realize my baby brother's got a reputation for being a bit of a playboy, but he takes his work seriously. I'm sure he'll have the child-care angle all figured out before he makes his first move. If Blake's anything, he's resourceful.'' He was silent a minute, as if to let his words sink in, and then one side of his mouth quirked up. ''Although I've got to admit, I'm sure this mission of his is going to have its moments. I'd like to be around the first time he has to change a diaper.''

''Yeah, there is that,'' Sterling agreed, his own mouth curving slightly at the thought—until it occurred to him that come next spring he'd be doing the same thing and his amusement vanished.

The two men spoke a few more minutes about local business before Greg drained his glass, set it down on the table and climbed to his feet. ''Well, I need to get going. I have a pile of briefs I need to go over tonight.'' He cocked his head. ''So when am I going to meet your bride? I was pretty sure I knew everybody in this town, but somehow she passed me by.''

That, at least, wasn't a bit surprising. The Hunts were old money; Greg probably hadn't had a reason to set foot in a public library since law school. ''Soon,'' Sterling replied, repeating his answer to Becky. ''We're thinking of having a reception. I'll let you know.''

''You do that.'' With a nod, Greg departed.

As Sterling watched the other man walk toward the door, he found himself thinking how much things had changed. The last time he'd seen Greg his life had been empty, and he'd been so restless and dissatisfied with it that he'd had nothing better to do than take off to Europe and come to a perfect stranger's rescue.

Now, his life seemed too full. And though he still felt

restless and dissatisfied, at least he knew the reason why, he thought sardonically.

Just like that, the dam he'd been keeping on his feelings finally let loose and he found himself thinking about what had transpired between him and Susan.

He could put any spin on it he wanted, but the truth was that one touch of her lips and the control he prided himself on had vanished.

Aw, come on. It was only a kiss…

But it hadn't been. By the time she'd made that soft little sound that had inexplicably gotten his attention, the only thought in his head had been whether it would be better to make love in the hammock or on the picnic table.

So? You didn't do it either place. And *that's* what matters—isn't it?

Well, yeah. That was true. But it sure hadn't been from any nobility of spirit. Because what he'd *wanted* to do was lay her down on the nearest horizontal surface and bury himself inside her. He'd wanted to kiss her round little breasts, suck on her nipples, taste every inch of her ivory skin. Hell, he still wanted to do all those things, he admitted, scowling at the heaviness in his loins.

Yet what he'd told her was true. It *was* too soon. If he slept with her now, he was pretty sure she'd get the wrong idea. She'd give it all sorts of romantic significance, or even worse, she'd start to think she was in love with him. And then later, when she realized that he was never going to love her back, when she learned that he was done with such feelings, she'd feel hurt and betrayed—and then where would they be?

Better by far to wait and give them more time to get to know each other. Susan was an intelligent woman.

Sooner or later she would figure out what everyone else had—that he wasn't the "loveable" type. Then, if she still wanted to be intimate, so much the better.

Because, while he might not love her, he was fond of her, he realized. She was smart, sensible and kind, and he liked her understated sense of humor. She was also surprisingly easy to live with, a rarity for a woman in his experience. Hell, if not for this unfortunate physical attraction between them, she'd be the perfect wife.

Which made him realize he was probably doing her a disservice. By now she would've had time to reflect on what had happened between them. And because she was such a nice person, she was no doubt not only regretting her behavior, but also sorry she'd put him in such a tough position. If he gave her half a chance, she'd probably say so.

But that's where it was going to end, he promised himself. He'd made a vow to never again let a woman matter to him too much—and he meant to keep it. Somehow today, he'd lost control and let Susan get past his defenses.

It wouldn't happen again.

He wouldn't let it.

Fresh and fragrant from her bath, Susan stood before her bedroom window, wrapped in an oversize bath towel. Looking down, she saw the beam from a pair of headlights flash across the back pasture, then abruptly disappear. A second later came the faint sound of a car door slamming shut.

Sterling was home.

She instinctively touched her hands to her stomach as it fluttered nervously. She could do this, she told herself. All she had to do was stay calm.

She'd had lots of time to think since their aborted embrace out by the lake. She'd reflected on her actions, on what had happened and what Sterling had said about it afterward. And she'd come to a conclusion.

He was wrong.

It was not too soon for them to make love. Not if that's what they both wanted. After all, as she'd tried to point out to him earlier, neither of them were children. And in her case, at least, it wasn't as if she were rushing into anything. In a year and a half, she'd be thirty. She'd waited a long time to find someone she desired—and someone who desired her.

Which Sterling did. She smiled, unable to help herself as the realization sent a little thrill through her, the way it had off and on ever since it finally occurred to her on the walk back to the house. She might still be a virgin—heck, she was probably the only twenty-eight-year-old one left in the entire state of Texas—but she wasn't deaf, blind or stupid. She knew that Sterling had been as affected by their encounter as she had. He hadn't been acting polite, or merely going through the motions.

He wanted her, thank heavens.

And she wanted him back.

However, it also seemed very clear from what had happened out at the lake earlier that she'd be a virgin forever if it was left up to Sterling. She wasn't quite sure what the problem was. Knowing him as she was beginning to, she suspected it had something to do with his strong sense of responsibility and that it was likely he was trying to protect her.

From what, she didn't have a clue. But it did seem obvious that the only way anything was going to happen was if she made the first move.

That she was prepared to do. Turning away from the

window, she tugged the towel free and let it drop to the floor. She opened her top dresser drawer and drew out the filmy black lace chemise the saleslady from Cachet had insisted she purchase. Slipping it over her head, she smoothed it into place, stepped into the matching bikinis, then picked up her hairbrush and drew it through her hair. Only then did she look in the mirror.

Her lips parted in surprise. Surely that wasn't her! Thanks to the touch of makeup she'd applied in the bathroom—a smudge of eyeliner, a hint of mascara, a dusting of blush and a coating of strawberry lip glosser— her eyes looked huge and her lips full and smooth. As for the scanty ebony nightie… The shirred top clung to her like a second skin, making her breasts look as if they might spill free any moment, while the abbreviated length made the most of her legs.

She swallowed. Then, a rueful expression crossing her face, she opened the dresser drawer and drew out the robe that went with the chemise. Slipping her arms into the sheer sleeves, she reminded herself that Rome wasn't built in a day. And that she was doing okay for a woman who until a few weeks ago had slept in an old Dallas Cowboys T-shirt.

She spritzed herself with a touch of perfume and took a deep breath, feeling a return of her confidence.

She was ready. Before she could lose her nerve, she walked into the dressing area that bridged her and Sterling's rooms and knocked lightly on his door.

There was no answer. Frowning, she considered, and concluded that he'd had plenty of time to get to his room. Afraid her newfound courage would desert her if she waited any longer, she knocked again, opened the door and stuck her head in. "Sterling?" she called softly.

He was standing barefoot at his dresser. At the sound of her voice, he whipped around and she saw that his shirt was open and his jeans unsnapped. An apology instinctively sprang to her lips, but she forced herself to suppress it. He was getting undressed; so much the better. It would make things easier later.

He turned back around and finished emptying his pockets, dropping his keys and his money clip onto the dresser. "Hey, Susan." His deep voice was even. "What can I do for you?"

She proceeded into the room. With her newfound awareness, she saw the way the skin across his nose and cheekbones tightened as he glanced over and took in her state of dress. And how his big body went taut, as if he were suddenly in a high state of tension.

That was only fair, she decided, since the sight of his bare chest and abdomen were making her feel warm and light-headed. She took a deep breath. "I was hoping we could talk."

He hesitated a bare instant, then nodded. "Sure. I kind of figured there were some things you might want to say to me."

She felt an overwhelming sense of relief. Apparently she'd misjudged him. He wasn't going to be difficult about this after all. "First, I want you to know how much I appreciate everything you've done the past few weeks," she said softly. "I know it can't have been easy. After all, I chose to have this baby. I thought about it, saved for it, planned for it. But you had the whole thing just handed to you, and even so, you've tried really hard to do the right thing."

He shrugged. "It's no big deal."

"It is to me. It's made me think about my life, about

what I want. And what I want—'' she took a calming breath ''—is for us to have a real marriage.''

Sterling was shaking his head before she finished. ''You don't mean that.''

''Yes, I do.'' Screwing up her courage, she closed the distance between them, not stopping until she was so close she could feel the heat radiating off of him. ''I realize I'm shy on experience,'' she went on quietly, tipping back her head so she could see his face. ''And that this has all happened very quickly. But that doesn't change how I feel.''

''You haven't thought this through,'' he insisted, taking a step back. ''Hell, we're still getting to know each other.''

''I know what I need to, Sterling. I know what a good person you are. And I know that you make me feel things I've never felt before.''

''Well, that's great.'' He made it sound anything but. ''What happened to our being friends? Do we just forget about that and settle for being lovers?''

''No, of course not. I don't see that one cancels out the other. If anything, our being intimate would probably help our friendship.''

''Oh yeah? And how do you figure that?''

''Because it should relieve some of the tension between us. Before, I thought it was just me. But then, today, down by the lake I realized that you felt it, too. And that I'd really like to be your lover before I become a mother.''

''Susan—'' he protested.

''I know what I'm asking, Sterling.'' Again she closed the distance between them. Laying her hand on a warm patch of skin exposed by his shirt, she echoed the shudder that shivered through him at her touch. ''Please. Make love to me.''

Eight

Sterling looked from Susan's upturned face to the small elegant hand that felt like a brand on his skin.

It wasn't fair. She had no right to put him through this. Not twice in the same day.

Because there was no denying the drumbeat of need pounding through him. He wanted her, so much that his skin felt tight and his muscles ached with the effort of not reaching for her.

As for his mind, it felt painfully split. *Go on,* urged a part of him. *She knows the score and she wants you anyway.*

Not to be denied, the other half counseled, *Stop this now, while you can. Be a man and walk away.*

"Oh, dear." Susan's soft voice, uncertain after what he vaguely realized had been an extremely protracted silence, intruded on the struggle he was waging with himself. "I thought—that is I assumed—I thought you wanted me, too. But you don't, do you?'' She started to draw her hand away. ''Oh, dear. I'm so sorry...''

He looked down and saw the hurt she was bravely trying to hide. And just like that, the decision was made. He still had reservations, but there wasn't one of them worth the look on her face. ''No. Don't be sorry.'' He caught her hand and deliberately guided it back to his chest. Pressing her cool palm against his hot skin, he had to grit his teeth at the jolt of pleasure that went through him. ''You weren't wrong,'' he said harshly. ''I just—you have to be sure, Susan. I don't want to hurt you.''

''Oh, Sterling. You'd never do that.''

He shook his head at her naiveté. ''Maybe not deliberately, but—'' he paused, his frustration manifesting itself as a muscle jumped in his jaw ''—you've got to understand. I want you. That's true. But I'm not in love with you.''

''I know. And it's all right,'' she said quietly. She stared up at him, the truth of what she was saying clear in her big brown eyes. ''I trust you.''

As if the moment was frozen in time, he registered a quartet of small details. The softness of her palm against his skin. The tantalizing familiarity of her scent. The darkness of her eyes. The pinkness of her lips.

Misunderstanding his silence, she reached up and laid the fingers of her free hand against his cheek. ''It really is all right, Sterling,'' she repeated.

Something inside him seemed to shatter. Desire—and a deeper need that was totally unexpected—roared through him. Before he could change his mind, he hauled her close, lifted her off her feet and took her mouth with his own.

The hours since their embrace at the lake might never

have happened. Instead of starting over, the passion between them returned full-force. Sterling felt it cut through him like a blow torch, burning away the last of his reservations.

She's right, he told himself. It was okay. He wasn't breaking his vow—not really. As Susan had pointed out, this was just physical desire. He wasn't giving her his heart or making a promise that he couldn't—he wouldn't—keep.

She had a point about a sexual liaison improving their relationship, too. Right from the beginning, he'd been negatively influenced by his attraction to her. If he could finally slake his hunger for her, get it out of his system once and for all, maybe he'd be able to get his life back the way he liked it—which was firmly under control.

At the moment, that was not an option. Driven by need, he began to walk blindly toward the bed, not stopping until he felt the edge of the mattress press into the backs of his legs. He tore his mouth from Susan's, and lowered her to her feet, his stomach hollowing as her body rubbed against his in the process. Trailing his fingers over her satiny-soft shoulders, he tugged off her robe and tossed it to the floor. A shudder went through him as he looked down at the soft thrust of her breasts straining the lace of her bodice. "Damn, but you're pretty."

"So are you," she said breathlessly, pushing at his shirt. When he looked at her sharply, her cheeks suddenly turned pink, but she didn't back down. "Well, you are."

Tenderness shot through him, tempering some of his urgency. He shrugged his shirt away. "Come here," he said hoarsely, sinking down on the bed and drawing her into the cradle of his thighs. "Touch me."

He didn't have to ask her twice. Her hands, tentative at first, traced the line of hair bisecting his chest and grazed the curls under his armpits. Quickly growing bolder, she ran her thumbs over his nipples. Her eyes rounded slightly as they drew into tight little beads. With a soft "oh," she stroked them again, then slid her palms down his sides, over his hipbones and across his abdomen. Bracing her fingers against the ridged muscle of his belly, she caught him off guard as she bent down and kissed his shallow navel.

Sterling's heart seemed to jump into his throat. He groaned, fighting the urge to tangle his hands in her hair and direct her attentions lower. *Easy,* he ordered himself. *Don't forget that she's new to this. And that she's carrying your child. Take it slow.*

Still, the urge to touch her, to lie down naked beside her, was riding him too hard to ignore any longer. He gently tugged her upright. He came to his feet, unzipped his jeans and pushed them and his briefs to the floor. Stepping free of the fabric, he heard Susan draw in her breath.

"Oh, my," she murmured. Her gaze shot to his face. "I know everything is supposed to be bigger in Texas, Sterling, but I—I don't think this is going to work."

Her words caught him by surprise. To his shock, he felt a grin tug at his face. Although it came and went in a flash, it served to increase the odd mixture of passion and protectiveness she was causing in him. "It'll work. I promise." Reaching for her hands, he tugged her onto the bed, turning at the last minute so she was underneath him.

"Shouldn't I take off my nightgown?" she said faintly.

"In a minute." He grimaced at the strain in his voice,

wondering if she had a clue just how much he wanted to strip her bare and plunge himself inside her. Yet her sudden nervousness was obvious and he wanted this to be good for her. He wasn't sure why it mattered so much, but it did. Leaning over, he kissed her, determined to rebuild her passion to match his own.

It didn't prove hard to do. Cupping her face in his hands, he plied her lips with his mouth. He nipped her lower lip and worried it with his teeth, and when she probed at the tiny hurt with her tongue, he sucked it into his mouth. He swallowed her faint cry of surprise. It quickly became a murmur of pleasure.

She was a quick study. Locking her hands around his neck, she dragged him closer, slanting her lips against his. Slowly at first, and then with more and more confidence, she began to imitate what he'd done to her out by the lake, making love to him with her mouth until they were twisting restlessly against each other.

He felt his control slipping away. Determined to get it back, he forced himself to break off the kiss. He looked down at her, watching as her heavy-lidded eyes rose to his. "Easy," he murmured, struggling for breath. "There's no rush."

She shook her head and tried to draw him back down to her. When that didn't work, she shifted impatiently and bent one silky leg, rubbing it against his hip and along his outer thigh before hooking it around his leg.

Perspiration sprang up across his forehead and in the small of his back. With a groan, he buried his face in her throat, fighting for restraint as her lace-covered hip rubbed tantalizingly against his straining sex. "Aw, sweetheart, please. Slow down. You're doing me in."

"Good," she said breathlessly. And then, "Don't stop."

He was powerless against her soft plea. Tangling his fingers in the dark fire of her hair, he sank his mouth into the vulnerable flesh at the base of her throat. She gave a muffled cry and he slid lower, closing his hand around one thrusting breast while his lips claimed the other. Fitting his mouth to her nipple, he began to suckle.

She cried out again. Then, with a strength he hadn't known she possessed, she wrapped her arms around him and shifted, centering herself beneath him. Clamping his hips in her knees, she tangled her hands in his hair and fit herself against his hardness.

Wild fire. Sterling felt the heat of it in his blood. Raising his head, he tugged down her bodice, unable to stop the sound that tore from his throat as her breasts popped free, exposing small, stiffly erect peach-colored nipples. Leaning down, he raked one with his teeth.

She whimpered and rocked herself against him.

He swallowed a curse. She was driving him wild, and suddenly, he just had to touch her. His mouth against her breast, he twisted, rolling them onto their sides. Reaching down, he pushed her nightie out of the way and placed his hand between her thighs, rotating his thumb over her satin-covered mound.

She bucked as if she'd been touched by a live wire. "Sterling!"

"Do you like that?"

"Yes. Oh, yes!"

He kissed his way to her mouth and stroked her again, touching her until he felt a growing circle of damp against his fingertips. "That's right," he said against her lips.

She shuddered. "Oh! That feels—I didn't know... I need... Oh, Sterling, please!"

He couldn't wait any longer.

Coming up on his knees, he gripped the hem of her gown and dragged it up and over her head. On some level he registered how exotic her pale skin and dark flame hair looked against the royal-blue of his satin bedspread. It was too much; he looked away, his self-control balanced on a razor's edge as he gripped her black satin panties and pulled them away.

He moved between her thighs.

Susan stared up at him. Rising above her, he looked like every red-blooded woman's dream. The muscles in his arms and torso were hard with tension, his eyes were heavy-lidded, his lips still wet from their kisses. The bronze tones of his skin were in sharp contrast to her own paleness, while a single lick of dark brown hair fell forward, softening the hard angles of his face.

Emotions flooded her: tenderness, excitement, desire. She reached up. Brushing back that silky strand of hair, she looped her hand behind his neck and drew him down for an openmouthed kiss, only to gasp at the sensation as they came together, fully naked for the first time. His hard, hot chest rubbed against her sensitive nipples, while lower down his muscled abdomen pressed between her thighs. He felt impossibly heavy. But so very good.

She felt the thrust of his tongue, the stabbing rhythm evoking the act to come. A second later, he shifted his lower body and touched her, rotating his thumb against the seat of her desire. He gently slid one big finger between her slick folds.

The shock of it jolted through her.

Before, the thought of a man touching her *there* had always seemed shocking, too intimate and invasive to bear.

With Sterling, it just felt right. Her entire world

seemed to narrow to the pleasure brought by his skillful fingers. He stroked her again and again, until her back was bowed and she was rocking mindlessly against his hand. Yet as good as it felt, it wasn't enough. She wanted more. She wanted *him*. "Sterling?"

"Hmm?" He was breathing hard.

"I want you inside me," she whispered.

For a moment he didn't move, and she was afraid she'd said something wrong. Her apprehension evaporated, however, as he shifted and his weight abruptly pressed her into the mattress. "Me, too," he murmured against her throat.

Bracing himself with an arm on either side of her, he lifted himself up. She felt the thick end of his sex nudge against her. For a moment she was convinced she'd been right, that this would never work. Yet inch by inch her body yielded to his. And though there was some pain, there was also a slow-building sense of anticipation as he gently, carefully filled her until she couldn't stand it any longer. "Don't," she bit out finally, straining against him.

He froze. "Don't what?"

"Don't go—so—slow. I need...I want...to feel all of you."

He groaned. "Susan. Sweetheart..."

That was the second time he'd called her sweetheart. The endearment shivered through her, the sweetest word she'd ever heard. "Please, Sterling. Do it harder. I promise I won't break."

"Hell, I know that. But I don't want to hurt you. Or the baby—"

"You won't." Reaching up, she gripped his bulging biceps and flexed against him, trying to draw him deeper. Then, with an instinct she hadn't known she possessed, she rotated her hips.

She felt the muscle beneath her fingers compress as his whole body tensed. Yet if there was one thing she was coming to understand about Sterling, he was nothing if not stubborn.

Gritting his teeth, he withdrew just a little before he pushed back into her. His thrust was harder this time, the angle not nearly so shallow, yet it was still carefully controlled.

"More," she demanded, laboring toward something just out of reach. "Please."

"In a minute—"

"No, now." Breathless, needy, and more than a little desperate, she thrust her hips upward on his downstroke, seating him fully inside her.

"Dammit, Susan." His big body quivered. "Are you all right?"

"Yes. Oh, yes. It's just that I need...I need—" Driven by something she couldn't contain, she reached down and clutched the hard curve of his buttocks, grinding him against her. To her shock, pleasure rocketed through her, explosive and unexpected. She felt herself tighten around him, felt her inner muscles contract wildly, shattering her into what felt like a thousand pieces. "Oh! *Ohh!* Yes!"

Sterling said something harsh under his breath as her climax triggered his own. With a guttural cry, he wrapped his fist in her hair and came, his big body shuddering convulsively at the rhythmic gloving of her body.

Moments later, he collapsed beside her, nestling his sweaty face in the crook of her neck. Feeling the fine tremors that continued to shiver through him, Susan cradled him against her, gently stroking the damp feathers of his hair.

Happiness burned through her. For the first time, she truly felt like Sterling's wife.

The bedroom was filled with sunshine by the time Sterling awoke the next morning.

Careful not to disturb Susan who lay curled against him, he stretched, then shifted onto his back.

He thought about the night just past, about the two of them making love. They'd done it despite his reservations, his worries about the future, his bald admission that he wasn't in love with her. What's more, they'd done it not just once or even twice, but three times, most recently shortly before sunrise, when he'd kissed Susan awake, rolled onto his back and guided her on top of him.

It would be a long time before he forgot how she'd looked in that silvery light, with her head thrown back, her perfect little breasts thrust forward, her shot-with-fire hair swaying as she rode him to another explosive climax.

And though he was pretty sure it didn't speak well of his character, he didn't regret one single moment of making love to her. Because as humbling as it was to admit it, sometime during the night a part of him that he'd refused to even acknowledge was wounded had been healed.

Now, lying here in a golden blaze of daylight long after the fact, he could finally admit to the hit that his ego had taken when Teresa had left him because he couldn't get her pregnant. And though he knew damn well that nothing could fix the more crucial flaw in his character that had prevented her and his mother—the only two people he'd ever loved—from loving him back, last night had nevertheless gone a long way toward alleviating that other, very masculine hurt.

Not to put too fine a point on it, but he felt good.

And he owed it all to Susan. Shy, inexperienced, kind-hearted little Susan, who'd given him far more than her virginity last night.

He turned his head on the pillow and looked at her sleeping face. Even with her lips swollen from his kisses, her cheeks pink from his beard and her hair tumbled wildly around her, she had a certain sweet serenity that appealed mightily to him. And though he didn't love her—he couldn't, and wouldn't, for both their sakes—he had to admit that last night had changed things between them.

Pure and simple, she belonged to him now in a way she hadn't before. While he'd felt protective from the beginning, it had been more about the child she was carrying than Susan herself. That was no longer true. Although he knew it was primitive, the intimacy of what they'd shared and the knowledge that he'd been her first and only lover, made him feel strongly that she was now *his*.

He'd take good care of her, he promised himself. He might not love her in a romantic sense, but her happiness did matter to him. He'd make sure she didn't regret what had happened between them.

Next to him, she stirred. He watched as her lashes slowly swept up and she took stock of their intimate position. Her gaze flickered down to the sheet-covered leg she had hooked over his, then up to her hand, which was possessively splayed across his bare abdomen. From there, it was just a matter of time before she took note of the way her bare breasts were pressed intimately against his side.

For a moment she didn't move. Then, taking him by surprise, she lifted her head and gently pressed a lingering kiss to his shoulder.

A fierce tangle of emotion twisted through him. He must have made a sound, because her gaze suddenly rose to his face. "Oh." The color in her beard-chafed cheeks deepened slightly. "You're awake."

"Yeah." To his chagrin, he found he had to clear his throat. "As a matter of fact, I am."

There was an awkward moment as they considered each other, and then she surprised him again with a shy, sudden smile. "I've never done this before—woke up with a man. Is there something I'm supposed to say?"

Some of his tension melted away. "No. You can do or say whatever you want to."

"Oh. Well then…" She didn't hesitate. Pushing herself up, she slid her hand around his neck and found his mouth for a brief but melting kiss. Raising her head, she smiled again. "Good morning," she said a little breathlessly.

Incredibly he found himself smiling back. "Yeah. It's turning out that way."

She settled back into the curve of his arm and for a space of time they simply laid there in surprisingly companionable silence. Finally, however, Susan said, "This is nice."

He nodded. "Yeah, it is."

"Do you know what time it is?"

He glanced over at the clock on his dresser. "A quarter after nine."

"Ah." For a few seconds the information didn't appear to really register. And then her head abruptly came up. "Oh, dear. I'm late for work."

"Forget work," he said, tightening his hold on her.

"I can't," she protested, misunderstanding. "Not until they find a replacement—"

"Relax. That's not what I meant. I'm not talking about quitting. I just thought maybe you could take today off and we'd spend it together."

Her eyes widened slightly. "You did?"

He smoothed a strand of silky auburn hair behind her ear. "Yeah."

"I'd like that." Her face lit up, only to dim an instant later.

"What's the matter?"

She hesitated, then said with obvious reluctance, "It's just… I'm not sure what you have in mind, but I'm afraid I'm starting to get a little tender—"

"Shh." He pressed a finger to her lips to stop her. "Don't worry about it. I didn't mean in bed."

Some of the worry left her face. "You didn't?"

"No." It was only a little lie. And when he stopped to think about it, he realized it really didn't matter. Although unwilling to examine his feelings too closely, what he wanted, what he needed, was just to be with her. "I'd like nothing better than to spend the whole day making love to you," he said truthfully, an idea taking shape in his head, "but what I have in mind actually works better with your clothes on."

"All right." She waited a heartbeat for him to say something. When he didn't, she said, "Are you going to tell me what it is?"

He shook his head. "No. I think I'll surprise you."

She considered him for a moment, then nodded. "Okay."

Once again he was struck by her unexpected trust in him. For the life of him, he couldn't decide if it was good or bad.

Nine

Sterling's surprise turned out to be a trip to Dallas.

To Susan's amazement, in the amount of time it took her to shower and pack an overnight bag, he'd made all the arrangements. By eleven they were aboard the Churchill Enterprise's Learjet and in the air. They landed at Love Field, where they were met on the tarmac by a chauffeured limousine that whisked them into the heart of the city. After a relaxing lunch at the fashionable Casa Renaldo's, they spent the rest of the afternoon shopping, making stops at Neiman Marcus, Ballinger's and Christian Maxwell, until Susan finally protested she couldn't possibly look at another thing.

With the exquisite care he'd shown her all day, Sterling promptly summoned the limo and some thirty minutes later the manager of the city's most exclusive hotel personally ushered them into the plush penthouse suite. Succumbing to exhaustion, Susan took a nap while

Sterling watched a Cowboy's game. Later, after showers and a visit from the hotel masseuse, they got all dressed up and had dinner on their own private, rooftop terrace, attended by a small army of white-coated waiters.

Now, curled up next to Sterling on the sitting room couch, the lights of Dallas spread out below them like a sequined cloak, Susan gave a deep sigh of contentment.

"You okay?" Sterling inquired, tracing a circle on her bare shoulder with his fingertips.

"Mmm-hmm. I'm fine. Why?"

"You've gotten pretty quiet all of a sudden."

"Have I?" She smoothed her palm over the exquisitely soft burgundy velvet of her evening dress, then looked up at him and smiled. "I guess I was just thinking that it's been a Cinderella kind of day. And that any second now I'm going to wake up in my little house back in Royal and this will all be a dream."

"I hope that means you had a good time."

She gave a happy sigh. "Oh, yes. It's been wonderful. Except that I keep expecting Robin Leach to pop up from behind a chair and announce we're on *Lifestyles of the Rich and Famous.*"

"He'd better not," he said lightly. Reflected light from the candles illuminating the room danced in his eyes, turning them to silver. "Not when I've finally got you all to myself. I didn't think that maid was ever going to leave."

"I know. Wasn't it amazing? I've never been anywhere where they turned down the bed, much less sprinkled it with rose petals, left chocolates on the pillows and offered to show up in the morning to draw your bath."

"Yeah. Pretty damn annoying, huh?"

She glanced over at him and shook her head, deliberately trying to look prim. "You're just spoiled."

To her delight, the corners of his mouth turned up in a faint but definite grin. "Well, I'm not sure about that. But I'm working on it."

His smile, still such a rarity, seemed to go right through her. And though she told herself the sudden rush of happiness she felt was nothing unusual, that she was just glad he was enjoying himself, she was no longer sure that was entirely true. As much as she'd enjoyed today, it had been last night that had been truly special. And while she'd meant every word that she'd said about being able to accept that he desired rather than loved her, her own feelings for him no longer seemed quite so simple.

Yet there was no way she could say so. Not now, she thought, glancing vacantly down at the belated engagement ring he'd insisted on buying her. It simply wouldn't be fair. Not after she'd insisted she was an adult who knew what she was doing a scant twenty-four hours ago. And not when he'd gone to such trouble to make the day—and the evening—so perfect and memorable.

Oblivious to her troubled thoughts, he continued his unexpected teasing. "What's the matter? Having second thoughts already? Wishing you'd let me buy you the ring I wanted to, instead of that little thing?"

"Absolutely not." To her relief, her voice sounded normal. With a determined smile, she held out her hand to admire the exquisite but tastefully sized emerald solitaire now nestled against her wedding band. "This ring is perfect. Not that the other one wasn't nice, too," she was quick to add. "But the diamond was just so...huge." Her eyes twinkling, she gave him a pointed sideways look. "I was afraid one of the horses might mistake it for a sugar cube and bite off my finger."

He sighed with mock despair. "Very funny. You know, you may look as soft as a kitten, sweetheart, but deep down you're one tough customer. First you rejected my choice of jewelry. Then you went and added insult to injury by refusing to let me buy you a few measly clothes—"

"A few? Oh, Sterling!" She laughed softly. "That saleslady trotted out enough stuff to dress an army!"

"So?"

"So just where in Royal was I supposed to wear a pantsuit trimmed in lavender ostrich feathers? Or a pair of faux leopard pedal pushers?" Not waiting for his answer, she added, "And I did let you buy me this." She touched the high-cut bodice of her evening dress. "As for the rest... Considering that in a month or two I'm going to need maternity clothes, it would have been a terrible waste of your money."

"Hell, Susan, I can afford it. And you could always wear the stuff after you have the baby."

"I don't know about that," she said wryly. "I remember my mother telling me it took her a year to lose all the weight she gained with me. Of course," she added thoughtfully, "I was a pretty good size baby— eight pounds, two ounces, to be exact. What about you?"

He was silent a moment, then shrugged. "I don't know."

"You don't?" Susan didn't think to hide her surprise. "I guess we'll have to ask your mother."

Unexpectedly he shifted away from her, leaning forward to pick his wineglass up off the coffee table. He took an unhurried sip. "I don't want to disappoint you, but I doubt she remembers," he said finally.

She stared at his back. This wasn't her first indication that he didn't have the greatest relationship with his mother. And though he was always very careful not to say anything negative about her, his very neutrality spoke volumes. Whatever the problem, it went deep.

And that troubled her. Gathering her courage, she leaned forward and gently rubbed her hand against the base of his spine. "I'm sure that's not true. And even if it is, it's her loss—"

"You're right," he said, cutting her off. He settled back beside her, a trace of his old guardedness coloring his face. "But it's nothing you need to worry about. I don't want you worrying about anything," he stressed. "Not money or clothes or gaining weight—and certainly not my mother."

Susan stared at him, very aware that he'd just made a deliberate choice not to share an important part of himself with her. Yet before she could even think how to protest, he lifted her onto his lap. "And I'll tell you a little secret. As beautiful as you look right now—" he bent his dark head and nuzzled the exquisitely sensitive place behind her ear, his voice husky with emotion "—the thought of our baby growing inside you excites the hell out of me. I can hardly wait to see your body change."

His words caught Susan by surprise and took some of the sting out of his decision not to confide in her. "Oh, Sterling." Ambushed by tenderness, she pressed her lips to his hair, helpless to resist when a second later he tipped her back against his arm and his mouth found hers. Nor did she protest a few minutes later when he climbed to his feet with her in his arms and carried her into the bedroom.

As if she were made of glass, he set her gently on her feet next to the huge, canopied bed. He studied her the briefest of moments, then stood back and began to struggle with the jet studs on his shirtfront.

"Here. Let me." She brushed his fingers away and in no time at all he was bare-chested. Leaning forward, she pressed a kiss to his collarbone, her knuckles resting intimately against his taut abdomen as she undid the buttons on his tailored slacks.

Sterling sucked in his breath and caught her wrists as she fumbled for his zipper. "Hold on." Gently pushing her hands away, he sank down on the bed and tugged off his dressy black cowboy boots. He tossed them and his socks away and stood. His pants and briefs hit the floor a second later. Then he reached for Susan. "Darlin'," he drawled, "you are definitely overdressed."

Her heart melted at his unexpected playfulness. Before he could catch her, however, she stepped back, reached behind her, and unzipped her gown, pulling it over her head and tossing it away. Wearing nothing but her high heels and a pretty but conservative black satin bra and panty set, she smoothed back her hair and faced him. "Better?"

"You're getting there."

He took a step closer, but to her surprise, made no move to undress her further. Instead he went down on his knees. Cradling the soft swell of her hips in his hands, he leaned forward and reverently began to press a string of kisses across the curve of her stomach. He was infinitely gentle, and she shivered as she felt the cool strands of his hair tickle the underside of her breasts.

Still on his knees, he reached behind her, unhooked
her bra and pulled it away. He made a low sound of
appreciation as his hands came around and cupped her.
''God, you feel so good.'' Closing his eyes, he rubbed
one smoothly shaved cheek against a turgid nipple, then
turned his head and took the stiff little morsel in his
mouth.

The breath seemed to freeze in her throat. ''Oh,
my....'' Clutching his shoulders, she looked down at his
dark head, watching his cheeks flex as he suckled. Heat
curled through her. An ache bloomed between her thighs
and her knees began to tremble. ''Sterling...'' she said
helplessly.

He released her breast with a wet little sound. Yet she
got no relief as he trailed his hands down her middle,
hooked his thumbs in the top of her panties and tugged
them off. He leaned back, his eyes smoky as they took
in her distended nipples and the neat triangle of dark
curls atop her thighs. He swallowed. ''You're so pretty.''
He pressed an openmouthed kiss to her most intimate
place.

Susan swayed, only her grip on his shoulders keeping
her upright until he finally climbed to his feet. He urged
her toward the bed.

''Wait,'' she said softly. At his questioning look, she
gathered her courage. ''I...I want to touch you, too,
okay?''

His expression registered surprise, then a sort of wry
amusement. He shrugged his wide, bronzed shoulders.
''Sure.''

She hooked a hand around his neck and tugged his
head down. Shaping her mouth to fit his, she initiated a
series of slow, soft, coaxing kisses. He moved closer,
rubbing gently against her until she could feel the hot

ridge of his sex pressing against her stomach. Still clutching his neck, she reached down with her free hand and tentatively closed her fingers around him.

He felt hot, smooth and firm. Gripping him lightly, she rubbed her thumb across the broad tip, fascinated as she heard his breath catch and felt him jerk against her palm.

The kiss grew more intense. Reveling in her newfound power, she repeated the caress, once, twice, until suddenly, he tore his mouth from hers, reached down and carefully but firmly pulled her hand away.

Her gaze shot to his face. "What's the matter? Did I do something wrong?"

His throat worked. "No." He seemed to struggle for composure, then managed a strangled laugh. "But if you keep that up, things'll be over before they start."

"Oh."

He drew her onto the bed, scattering rose petals right and left as he rolled onto his back and lifted her astride him.

The intimacy of the position was startling. Susan tried to take it all in: the firm but gentle grip of his hands, the silky heat of his stomach against her thighs, the blunt head of his sex nudging against her a second before he slid solidly inside.

"Oh!" She arched her back, struggling to adjust to the full, stretching pressure.

"Easy," Sterling soothed. "There's no rush. You set the pace."

Bunching a pillow behind his head, he held himself still and it suddenly dawned on her that she was in charge. Leaning forward, she braced her hands on either side of his head and slowly raised her hips.

Carefully she sank back down, and felt a little tickle

of pleasure. Up again, then down, and the pleasure grew stronger. As it did, her hips began to move a little faster.

"Come here." Tangling his hands in her hair, Sterling brought her mouth to his and his own hips rose off the bed.

Tension began to build in her body. She rocked against him, taking him deeper, unprepared as her orgasm suddenly rushed through her in a crest of pleasure. She cried out, saying Sterling's name over and over.

He reached down, grabbed her hips and continued to thrust heavily into her. Out of nowhere, another explosion hit her, more powerful than the first. She felt Sterling stiffen, felt his body bow beneath her as his hands bit into her hips and he held her against him. Then he too was crying out, a deep guttural sound of completion.

Sobbing for breath, Susan collapsed against him. For a few seconds he didn't move. And then his arms came around her and he held her tight, and she felt him press a kiss to her hair.

And that's when she knew she loved him.

Late-afternoon sunlight danced on the surface of the Oasis swimming pool.

Sterling drove through the clear blue water, his path as straight and true as an arrow, his stroke powerful and steady. Approaching the wall, he made a perfectly executed racing turn and kicked off, heading back the way he'd come.

He wasn't sure how many laps this made. Ten? Twenty? It didn't matter. He felt as if he could go on forever.

He tried to remember the last time he'd had so much energy. Hell, it had to have been over a decade ago, toward the end of his stint in the military. He'd been in the best shape of his life, running ten miles every morning, working out for a few hours each evening.

Of course, he'd also been young, a little cocky, and away from home for the very first time in his life. Between hanging out with his buddies and dating one of the local beauties, he hadn't gotten a lot of sleep at night. Not that it had mattered.

He'd had energy to burn. Just like now.

Only he wasn't a kid anymore. And real life had done a lot to temper his youthful arrogance. And while he tried to stay in shape, he no longer had hours a day to devote to it.

About the only parallel between then and now was that lately he hadn't been getting a whole lot of sleep. And there was an obvious reason for that, he thought wryly.

His wife was keeping him up at night.

He smiled despite himself and completed another lap, then propelled himself into the middle of the pool. Breaking the surface, he flipped onto his back, blinked the water out of his eyes and stared up at the vast blue sky.

He had to admit, in the back of his mind he'd expected that once they'd made love a few times, some of the edge would be off his attraction to her. It didn't seem to be working out that way, however. She was so sweet, so responsive, so generous in her lovemaking that he couldn't seem to get enough of her.

As if that weren't surprise enough, he liked spending time with her out of bed, too. She had an inner serenity and a steadiness of character that made her easy to be around, and an unspoiled view of life he found refreshing. He couldn't remember the last time he'd enjoyed himself as much as he had on their trip to Dallas.

Unless it was the past few days. For the first time in years, he'd actually taken some time off from work. And since the library had finally found a replacement for Susan, they'd been able to spend quite a bit of time together. They'd gone on errands, begun to plan the baby's room, driven out to the Moran's to see Clarry and visit the puppy, now named Rosie, who would finally be ready to come home with them next week. Although it was the last thing he expected, Sterling had found that the more he did with Susan, the more he looked forward to her company.

Not that he needed her or anything, he was quick to assure himself. Hell, he didn't need anybody. He simply enjoyed being with her, that was all. And as Susan herself had pointed out, a strong bond between them was best for the baby…

Staunchly rejecting the errant thought that there might be more to it, he continued to float, his mind drifting like one of the wispy clouds high overhead, until the sound of approaching footsteps brought his head around.

"Hi." Susan, pretty in a pale green sundress and sandals and with her hair tied back, smiled at him. "You look like you're enjoying yourself."

"Yeah, I am."

"It's so hot. It's hard to believe it's already October."

"Yeah, I know." He made his way to the side of the pool, slicked his hair off his face with his hand and looked up at her. "I guess we'd better enjoy it while we can."

She nodded, her gaze sliding over him like an invisible caress.

"So what's up?" he asked.

"Oh." She looked up from her open admiration of his water-beaded chest. "I just came to remind you about my doctor's appointment. It's no problem if you'd rather stay here and laze around the pool—"

"No. I told you. I want to go." Bracing his hands on the coping block, he levered himself out of the pool. "It's not until four-thirty, right?" He climbed to his feet.

She picked up his towel off a chair and handed it to him. "Right."

He scrubbed the water from his hair and dried his face. Looping the towel around his neck, he glanced over at the clock on the cabana wall. It read three forty-five. "No problem. Give me twenty minutes to shower and dress and we'll be on our way."

"Okay," she said in her easy way.

He looked at her, the breeze gently ruffling her hair, and a strong surge of emotion went through him. Telling himself firmly that what he felt was simple fondness, and that his unwillingness to analyze it further was due to the need to get going, he nevertheless found time to give in to temptation. Leaning forward, he looped a hand around her neck and kissed her, careful not to get her dress wet.

When he finally straightened, her cheeks were flushed and her eyes a little dazed. "What was that for?" she asked faintly.

He shrugged. "Just because."

And yet as he headed for the house, he felt a little surge of uneasiness. Because deep down he recognized that he'd just done what he had out of an undeniable need to brand her as his.

The soft strains of a string quartet floated from hidden speakers, mixing with the soft hum of conversation that permeated Claire's, Royal's best—and only—French restaurant.

Susan set down her fork and sat back in her chair, unable to eat another bite of her dessert. Try as she might, she couldn't seem to conjure up much of an appetite. And the reason was sitting across from her.

Her doctor's appointment had gone smoothly. Due to her method of conception, this was the second time she'd seen Dr. Ross, a calm, cheerful man in his late forties. After answering a barrage of questions from Sterling, he'd given her a thorough examination, then assured them that everything seemed to be progressing normally. He'd told her he'd like to see her again in six weeks, and that had been that.

Yet Sterling had been markedly quiet ever since they'd left the doctor's office. Susan had tried repeatedly to draw him into conversation over the course of dinner with limited success. And though she tried to tell herself it was nothing, she couldn't seem to stop worrying about the cause.

"Sterling?"

"Hmm?"

"You're not disappointed are you?"

He set down his coffee cup and looked at her, one dark eyebrow rising. "About what?"

"The doctor's appointment. Because there'll be more to it on the next visit. We should be able to hear the baby's heartbeat. And Dr. Ross will probably do an ultrasound. I'm sure he would have done one today if the technician hadn't been working on the machine."

"Susan. I wasn't disappointed. Everything's fine. What's the matter?"

"It's just…you've been so quiet ever since we left

the doctor's office. I thought maybe something was bothering you.''

''No.'' He shook his head, although he still looked far too serious. ''Not at all.''

''Because I'd understand, I really would, if you were feeling bad because…because I'm the one who's pregnant.''

He gave an inelegant snort. ''As opposed to who? Me?''

She flushed. ''No, of course not. I meant—'' she took a deep breath ''—instead of Teresa.'' Heaven help her, but the words just sort of popped out. Yet the instant she said them she had to admit that the idea had been bothering her for a while.

He stared at her, his expression suddenly impossible to read. ''Why the hell would you think that?''

She gave a little shrug. ''You just never talk about her,'' she said slowly. ''And you obviously never would have gone to the clinic for help, much less married me, if having a child wasn't terribly important to you—''

''It is,'' he interrupted. He was silent a moment, then said more gently, ''That's the point. I guess it just hit me, that's all.''

''What?''

''That we're having a baby.'' His expression turned slightly rueful. ''I mean, I've known it all along in an abstract way. But somehow today, when the doc confirmed the due date and asked whether you wanted to deliver here at the clinic, or make the trip to Odessa or Midland, it suddenly seemed real. In a little more than six months, I'll be somebody's father.'' He hesitated a second, then reached across the table and lightly touched her hand with his own. ''As for Teresa…she's not my wife and she's not the one who's carrying my child. You are. And that's all that matters."

She smiled, feeling relieved, yet also aware that he hadn't said a word about how he felt about her. And though she knew she wasn't being fair, she couldn't deny she felt a slight sense of disappointment.

"Actually I've been thinking that it might be nice to have a party, sort of make our marriage official," he went on.

"I'd like that," she said sincerely.

"Good."

Across the room, a mixed party of six stood up from their table and began to make their way to the exit. They were partway across the room when one of the group, a good-looking man casually dressed in boots, jeans, sport coat and hat, glanced over and caught sight of them. A sudden smile lit up his lean, rugged face. He said something to his companions, then detached himself from the group and made a beeline for Susan and Sterling's table. "Hey, Church. I thought that was you." He stuck out his hand and Sterling rose to take it.

"Forrest. Good to see you." Handshake completed, he snagged an empty chair and pulled it over. "Have a seat."

"I've only got a minute." The newcomer sat, not trying to hide his curiosity as he glanced at Susan.

Following his gaze, Sterling made introductions. "Susan, this is my friend, Forrest Cunningham. I'm sure you've heard of his ranch, the Golden Steer."

"Oh, yes. Of course."

"Forrest, this is my wife, Susan."

The two exchanged polite greetings.

"I heard you got married," Cunningham said to Sterling. He shook his head. "I didn't believe it at first.

But now, seeing your bride here…'' He turned to Susan, his gaze admiring as he said with disarming charm, ''It's pretty obvious why he fell for you, ma'am.''

She smiled at the compliment. ''Why, thank you.''

''Truth to tell, I've been thinking about tying the knot myself, lately,'' he confided unexpectedly.

Sterling's eyes narrowed with surprise. ''I thought you liked being a bachelor.''

Forrest nodded. ''I do. But I'm not getting any younger. And that little trip I took to Europe recently got me thinkin', I guess.''

Before he could say more, one of the people from his party appeared in the door and waved, and he abruptly came to his feet. ''It appears I'm holding things up. It was good to see you, Church, and real nice to meet you, Susan.'' Tipping his hat to Susan, he was on his way.

''What a nice man,'' Susan said softly.

''Yeah, I guess,'' Sterling murmured thoughtfully, as he watched the other man leave the room. Turning back to Susan, an appreciative smile curved his mouth as he looked at her. ''I've got to admit, he does have better taste than I thought.''

They stared at each other. Susan felt a little shiver go through her as she saw the heat in his cloud-gray eyes.

''Did you get enough to eat?''

''Yes.''

''I don't know about you, but I'm ready to go home,'' he said quietly.

''Me, too.''

Without another word, he threw some money down on the table to cover the bill and stood, coming around to pull back her chair. With a proprietary hand to her shoulder, he guided her toward the door.

God help him, but he suddenly couldn't wait to get her alone.

Ten

"**C**ome here," Sterling said quietly, reaching for Susan as they entered his bedroom. Stroking his hands down her slender back, he pressed her against him and claimed her mouth, unable to wait another second.

On some level, he chafed at his urgency. Though he'd struggled not to let on, it had been riding him hard ever since their trip to the doctor's office. And though he'd stubbornly refused to give in to it, suggesting they eat dinner out just to prove to himself he could do it, the passage of time clearly hadn't done a damn thing to temper his need for her.

But then, while he'd told Susan the truth in the restaurant earlier when she'd asked him about his air of distraction, he hadn't told her the whole of it. He hadn't told her how, as he'd listened to her talk to the doctor, he'd been struck by an intense gladness that she was his child's mother. Or explained how much her honest joy in her pregnancy meant to him. And he sure hadn't volunteered that, for a few paralyzing moments, as the doctor had blandly discussed labor and delivery, he'd been struck by sheer terror at the thought that something might happen to her.

Nor could he explain why all those things together had seemed to translate into an intense need to take her to bed.

They just had.

In his arms, Susan gave a little shudder and broke the kiss. She gave him a curious look, then released a shaky laugh and leaned weakly against him, her hands splayed against his chest. "Wow. I keep thinking I'm not going to melt just because you kiss me," she murmured, rubbing her cheek against his shirtfront. "But so far, I'm not having much luck."

"Good." Catching her chin in his hand, he slid his mouth over hers and gently raked her bottom lip with his teeth. "Let's go to bed."

Instead of acquiescing the way he expected, she shook her head. "In a minute. First, I have something I want to give you."

"I have something I want to give you, too."

She laughed her gentle laugh. "I'm serious."

"Me, too." Nevertheless, his curiosity was aroused and he reluctantly let her go. "Okay. I've waited this long. I guess I can wait a few minutes longer."

With an air of anticipation, she headed for the inner door that led to her bedroom. In a minute she was back. In her hands was a large, flat package. It was beautifully wrapped in dark blue foil paper and tied with a thin gold ribbon.

He looked at her in surprise. "What's this?"

"I told you. It's for you."

He looked from the package to her shyly smiling face, not about to admit that he'd assumed her "gift" was going to have something to do with killer lingerie. Suddenly he felt off balance. "Susan," he protested, "you shouldn't have bothered—"

"I wanted to. You've given me so many lovely things. I wanted to give you something back."

"You already have. The baby—"

"No." Shaking her head, she held out the package. "That's not the same. This is just from me to you."

He gave her a long look. Then, without further ceremony, he took it, pulled off the ribbon and tore away the paper.

He looked down at her offering.

It was an enlarged photograph of a horse, beautifully matted and placed in an elegant silver frame. Not just any horse, he suddenly realized, looking more closely, but his very own Cassie. Obviously taken in the mare's prime, the photo captured her beautiful spirit as she ran full out across a pasture, her head and tail up, her mane floating on the air, her legs beautifully extended. In the moment caught on film, she seemed the embodiment of joy.

"I know it's not much," Susan said anxiously at his continuing silence. "But I thought you might enjoy having it."

"Where—" To his chagrin, his voice was thick with emotion. "Where did you get it?"

"Your friend Becky dropped by one day last week. We talked, and I told her what I had in mind, and she gave me the name of Cassie's original owners. I called and they were happy to send along a bunch of snapshots. This was my favorite."

He walked over and set it carefully on his dresser. "I can see why."

"Then you like it?"

Sterling glanced over at her. The photo was something he'd cherish always. But more than that, he couldn't remember the last time anyone had given him a present, much less taken such time with one. The fact that she had made him feel funny. Grateful and inexplicably uncomfortable all at the same time.

He cleared his throat. "Yeah. I do. A lot."

The words seemed woefully inadequate. Frustrated, he took refuge in action. Closing the distance between them, he cupped her face in his hands and kissed her, willing her to understand what he didn't have the words to say.

For Susan, all the worries of the day seemed to fall away as she saw the look in his eyes the moment before his mouth touched hers. Kicking off her sandals, she came up on tiptoe. She rested her hands against his chest and kissed him back for all she was worth.

The passion between them went from ember to flame in a heartbeat.

He made a sound deep in his throat. Tugging loose the scarf she'd used to tie back her hair, he thrust his fingers into the silky softness, tipped back her head and slid his open mouth along the satiny column of her throat. Seconds later, his hands found her zipper and slid it down. On the way back up, he unhooked her bra and pushed it and her dress off her shoulders, then stripped off her panties.

Faster than she could blink, he was out of his own clothes. He took her hand and tugged her toward the bed.

"Hey," she said breathlessly. "Where's the fire?"

He gave a hoarse laugh, but there was nothing amused about the look in his pewter eyes. "I want to be inside you. Now."

His bald admission and his raw need, so unlike his usual control, made her blood race with excitement. "Yes. Oh, yes..."

The words were barely out of her mouth before the mattress dipped beneath his weight. Catching her hands with his own, he rolled her beneath him and settled himself between her thighs. Susan felt his sex nudge intimately against her.

A second later, his back hollowed and he thrust, sliding all the way inside her.

She shuddered at the look of satisfaction that came over his face as his body filled hers. Reaching up to clutch his rock-hard biceps, she brought up her knees and lifted her hips to bring him deeper.

He braced himself on his elbows and caught her face in his hands. He nipped her bottom lip, worrying it beneath his teeth, and Susan moaned, shocked as she found that sharp little hurt seemed to intensify her pleasure. Faster and faster they rocked together.

"Aw, damn." His voice held a note of near-desperation. "I can't seem to get enough of you...."

It wasn't a declaration of love but in that moment it was more than enough. Her heart pounding, Susan arched into him as a rolling flood of pleasure caught her. Crying out, she clutched at his back and pressed her face into the crook of his neck. "I love you," she said breathlessly, unable to hold back the words any longer. "I love you so much."

The words pushed Sterling over the edge. Threading his fingers through hers, he pressed her into the mattress, his hips jerking uncontrollably. Dimly he heard himself

groaning and saying her name as his whole body began
to shudder and his climax slammed into him like a
sledgehammer.

It was a long time before he came back to himself.
When he did, all he could think of was the words she'd
said.

I love you.

Out of nowhere he felt a profound yearning to say it
back. Appalled at himself, he clamped his mouth shut.
And asked himself as he lay there, with Susan cradled
trustingly against him, what the hell he'd done.

Susan stood at the French doors in the kitchen early
the next morning. To the east, dawn was breaking. The
horizon was edged in gold, and ribbons of lavender and
pink were beginning to stretch slowly across the silvery
sky.

She barely noticed. Her attention was all for Sterling.

Unaware of her presence, he stood across the lawn at
the fence. Although she was sure a hint of the night's
chill remained in the air, he was barefoot, clad only in
an old pair of jeans. His bare arms were folded across
the top rail, his bare back hunched as he stared out at
something unseen. A few feet away, Cassie stood sentinel, one rear leg cocked in rest.

Susan felt a stirring of disquiet as she was struck by
how alone he looked.

She hadn't really thought much about it when she'd
awakened earlier and found him gone. Lying among the
tangled sheets, her body still tender from the previous
night's lovemaking, she'd simply assumed he was answering a call of nature. Yet as the minutes ticked past—
five, ten, twenty and then thirty—it had become clear

that wherever he was, he wasn't coming back anytime soon.

And still she hadn't been concerned. He'd been so full of energy lately that it hadn't seemed particularly odd that he might want to get an early start on the morning. So she'd stayed where she was a while longer before she finally climbed out from between the covers, slipped into her robe and made her way to the bathroom to freshen up.

When she walked into the kitchen, she'd expected to find him seated at the table, drinking a cup of coffee and reading the morning paper.

Instead the room had been empty. Perplexed, she'd been about to retrace her steps in search of him when a slight movement out in the yard had caught her attention.

That's when she'd seen him standing at the fence, half-naked and so starkly alone.

She bit her lip.

She supposed she ought to respect his privacy, pretend she hadn't seen him and go back upstairs. Yet something inside her balked. She knew instinctively that something was bothering him; even if this wasn't the very first time he'd ever left her to wake up on her own, she could see the tension in the rigid set of his shoulders. Besides, his self-imposed isolation simply felt all wrong.

Almost instantly, she found herself thinking about the previous day, about his silence after her doctor visit and the reason he'd given for it. At the time, his explanation had held the ring of truth. But now she wasn't so sure. *Did* he regret that he wasn't having this child with Teresa?

No, she decided a moment later. If that was how she truly felt, she was sure that somehow she would have known it. Sterling might not talk readily about his feelings, but he wasn't one to dissemble. She would have sensed his regret, or seen some sign of withdrawal.

And that certainly hadn't been the case last night, she thought, reassured as she recalled the urgency of his lovemaking.

But if that wasn't the problem, then what was?

She reviewed the rest of the evening. It didn't take long before she realized that the only other thing that had made last night different was that she'd finally told Sterling she loved him.

Her heart twisted in her chest.

She told herself sternly to stop borrowing trouble. After all, why would he find that disturbing? It wasn't as if she expected anything from him. And it wasn't as if she'd broken a promise or something...

Stop it, ordered a little voice in her head. *This isn't accomplishing anything. Chances are, the one has nothing to do with the other. For all you know, he's out there thinking about some thorny business deal. Or he's simply admiring the sunrise.*

But she'd never know if she stayed where she was.

Drawing herself up, she pulled the tie on her robe a little tighter and moved purposefully to the door. She pushed it open.

As she'd expected, it was cool outside. It was also very quiet. The same breeze that would be a steady rush by afternoon was now just barely stirring. And the only other sounds to be heard were the swish of the sprinklers running in a far pasture and the soft coo of the birds lodged in the trees out by the lake.

She crossed the patio and started across the lawn, trying to decide how to announce her presence only to find she didn't have to worry about it. As had happened several times in the past, when she was still several feet away Sterling seemed to know she was there. His head came up and he swiveled around. He gave her a brief look, then abruptly twisted back around.

His lack of a greeting spoke volumes.

Nevertheless, as she moved up beside him, she tried to pretend that everything was fine. "Hi," she said softly.

For a moment he said nothing. Then, still not looking at her, he said flatly, "What are you doing out here?"

She winced at his tone and forced herself to keep her own voice light. "I woke up and you were gone. When I came downstairs, I saw you from the window." She carefully rubbed Cassie's nose as the mare ambled over in greeting.

He shrugged. "I couldn't sleep."

"That's what I thought. Have you been up long?"

"Long enough."

There seemed no way to respond to that. She fell silent, fighting a sudden, overwhelming urge to retreat to the house, to respect his obvious desire to be left alone. And to avoid the confrontation that seemed to be brewing.

It was exactly what she would have done a month ago. Before she got pregnant. Before she got married.

Yet she wanted more for her child than a mother who was a coward, she reminded herself. Just as she wanted to be the best wife to Sterling she possibly could. And— she took a deep breath—she had a right to an explanation. After all, where would they be in the future if she let him shut her out the very first time there was a problem?

Gently she pushed Cassie away. "Sterling? What's the matter?"

He was quiet so long she didn't think he was going to answer. Finally however, he said, "Nothing."

"I see." She considered, then deliberately reached out and laid her hand on the hollow at the base of his spine. "Then come back to bed with me."

A muscle ticked to life in his jaw and he shook his head. "No. Not now."

"Why not?"

"Because."

His skin was warm and she slipped her hand a little lower. "Because why?"

He stiffened. "Don't, Susan."

"Don't what?"

Abruptly he turned to face her, dislodging her hand. "Don't push. It won't do any good."

"Then tell me what the problem is," she said quietly.

He gave her a long look, his gray eyes impossible to read. He seemed to come to some kind of decision. "All right. It's me." He shifted his gaze back out to the horizon. "I made a mistake. I let my desire for you get the best of my judgment, and I shouldn't have. I screwed up."

She answered without thinking. "No, you didn't—"

"Yeah, I did." His voice completely lacked emotion. "I knew you didn't have any experience. I knew you were too trusting, that you didn't have the kind of sophistication it takes to give your body to someone without thinking your heart was engaged. But I wanted you. And when you came and offered yourself to me, I convinced myself it would be okay."

"And it is," she said quickly. "I've never been so happy—"

"Maybe. But it won't last. It can't."

"Why not?"

"Because," he said almost gently, "you don't know me. Not really. Once you do, you'll understand."

"I know what I need to," she said firmly.

He shoved a hand through his hair with frustration. "No, you don't, Susan. Remember when you asked me if it bothered me that you were having my baby instead of Teresa? Well, I told you the truth—as far as it went. What I didn't say was that having a child was never my priority. It was important to Teresa," he stressed. "Not me. I'd have been happy to adopt. Or have it be just the two of us. But that wasn't enough for her. *I* wasn't enough for her."

Susan stared at him in dismay. And even as she decided that Teresa must have been a very stupid woman, an ache blossomed in her heart for his pain. He was a proud man, and such a rejection must have struck him hard. "But surely you can see that that's her problem. Her loss."

His expression turned sardonic. "I don't think so. I seem to have that effect on people." Seeing her open her mouth to protest, his face suddenly twisted. "Look— I'm sure you've caught on that my mother and I aren't exactly tight. That's because, try as she might, she never could warm up to me. Oh, she went through the motions, and she did her best to provide for me, but it was always duty, never love, and I knew it. Kids do." He shrugged. "That's just the way it was."

The ache in her heart intensified, but she knew better than to say anything. Later, she'd think about his mother, just as she'd let herself mourn for the child he'd been. But right now the look on his face warned that at the first sign of sympathy—which he'd no doubt mistake for pity—he'd close down and shut her out. "So? I'm not her. And I'm not Teresa—"

"Yeah, you're right. But you're also not me. And the bottom line is, I've learned my lesson. Love just isn't for me."

She struggled to hold onto her calm. "And what exactly does that mean?"

"It means you're a beautiful woman. You've got a good heart, and a lot of fine qualities that I admire, and I'm real glad you're going to be the mother of my child. If I was going to love anyone, it would be you. But I just don't have it in me. Not anymore."

Susan stared at him in disbelief. "But that doesn't make any sense. You have so much to give—"

"No. Not that way. Not anymore."

For a second she was so stunned, it was hard to take in what he was saying. She swallowed. "So what do you propose we do?"

"I think we need to take a step back. The reason we got married is so our baby would have a shot at a stable home with two parents to raise it—and that hasn't changed. I think we need to let things cool off and put the focus back on our being parents."

Susan gave him a long look, certain he couldn't be serious. "Just—just like that?"

"Yeah." It was clear from the stubborn set of his jaw that he meant it.

"But surely you can see—I can't just turn off what I feel for you like I would a spigot."

"You won't know until you try." Clearly done with the conversation, Sterling turned away and resumed his contemplation of the far horizon.

She looked up at his shuttered face. Feeling dazed, she realized she couldn't think what more to say.

She turned and walked away.

* * *

Sterling continued to stand at the fence long after Susan had gone. As the sun slowly rose higher, he began to feel the warmth of its rays against his face and chest.

Inside, however, he felt frozen. And it had nothing to do with the temperature.

He'd done the right thing, he told himself fiercely. Susan might not know it now, but later, when she got some perspective, she'd realize he'd done her a big favor. Better that she suffer a small hurt now rather than a bigger one later.

I love you, Sterling.

All right, he'd made a mistake, he conceded. He should have leveled with her from the start. But he was thirty-five years old and he couldn't change who or what he was. He'd done what he thought was best then, just as he was doing what he thought was best now.

The thing to remember was how much worse it would be if he'd let it go on.

He sighed, suddenly consumed with exhaustion.

Now all he had to do was figure out how to live with this crushing emptiness.

Eleven

"**I** don't want you to worry," Susan told Clarry, as the child escorted her and Sterling out of the Moran's house and to the truck. The afternoon sun sparkled on the vehicle's windows, while overhead not a cloud marred the vast baby-blue sky. "I promise we'll take good care of Rosie."

"Oh, I'm not worried. I trust Mr. Church." The little girl beamed devotedly at Sterling. "I know he'll love her and be the bestest dog owner ever. That's why I wanted him to have her. Oh, and you, too, Mrs. Church," she added artlessly.

The irony of the child's absolute faith in a certain tycoon wasn't lost on Susan. She glanced over at the man in question. To her surprise, instead of avoiding her gaze the way he had for the past five days, he was watching her, a brooding look on his face.

The moment their eyes met, however, he looked away.

"Well, we'd better get going," he said with deliberate heartiness. Reaching over, he opened the pickup's passenger door, then stood back and waited. Susan swallowed a sigh, climbed in and fastened her seat belt.

She watched as he mustered a smile, waited for Clarry to give Rosie one last kiss, then gently took the dog from the child's arms and handed the small animal to her. He shut the door without a word and gave Clarry's shoulder a final squeeze, before coming around the truck's hood and climbing into the driver's seat. The smile was gone from his face when he glanced at her. "You ready?"

She settled Rosie more securely on her lap. "Yes."

Facing forward, he started the truck and put it in gear. The second they cleared the yard, he reached for his cell phone, punched in a number and brought the instrument to his ear.

So much for taking a step back, Susan thought bleakly. This was the first time they'd been alone since that morning out by the fence, and so far it had counted for nothing. Sterling had spent every minute of the drive over on the phone, issuing instructions to an array of assistants. Now it appeared the drive home was going to be spent the same way.

He'd retreated so completely they might as well be living in separate countries.

She stared blindly out the window, feeling as desolate as the scenery flashing past. Except for the period after she'd lost her parents, the past few days had been the longest of her life. Although she was finally over the worst of her shock at Sterling's abrupt withdrawal, it seemed as if all she could do was think about him and what he'd said.

She'd analyzed, weighed, considered and replayed

every moment they'd ever spent together, only to confirm what she'd known in her heart all along.

He was wrong. Not just about the permanency of what she felt for him, she thought, idly petting Rosie's bumpy little spine. But about himself.

The man she knew wasn't incapable of love. Far from it. He might not carry his heart on his sleeve, but his actions spoke volumes. He was gentle, generous, responsible and caring. And no matter what he said, she knew he loved his home, his horses and his young friend Clarry. More than that, he loved a child that wasn't even born yet and—although he might refuse to admit, even to himself—she believed he loved her, at least a little. And though she felt both anger and anguish at what his mother and his ex-wife had put him through, allowing it to ruin their future together was wrong.

Of course, he was also incredibly stubborn. Each time she'd tried to talk to him this week, he'd made an excuse and bolted. And even so, she couldn't shake the idea that if they just spent some time together, he'd come to his senses and see how his actions were hurting them both.

She glanced over as he ended his call, then predictably began to dial another number. She bit her lip. If she had any moxie at all, she'd grab the thing and toss it out the window.

"Please don't," she said instead.

His hand froze in midmotion. He glanced over at her. "Sorry," he said levelly. "But I've got some business I have to take care of."

"I don't doubt you do. But we need to talk."

"I'm sure whatever it is can wait—"

"No, Sterling, it can't."

He was silent a moment. "All right," he said finally.

He flipped the phone shut and set it down on the console. "What is it you have to say?"

She turned toward him. "That I miss you. And that I can't go on like this, not talking, never seeing you—"

"Come on, Susan, you're overreacting. It hasn't been that long. And I can't help it if I'm busy. I let some things slide with the business to spend time with you last week and now I have to make up for it."

She stared at him in disbelief. "Are you saying it's *my* fault I haven't seen you?"

"Of course not. Just give it some time—"

"No." The puppy squirmed restlessly, as if sensing her distress. "I don't want to."

His hands tightened on the steering wheel, but his voice was excessively reasonable. "Look, I thought we agreed to take a step back, to reassess."

She shook her head. "I didn't agree to anything, Sterling. *You* made the decision, just like you decided we were going to get married and if we could be friends and whether or not we were going to make love. Besides—" try as she might, she couldn't keep the hurt out of her voice "—this isn't a step back. It's the biggest disappearing act since Houdini."

His jaw bunched. "All right. Maybe I overdid it. But I was just trying to make things easier for you. I thought you'd want some space. If that's not the case, I'm sorry."

She felt a stirring of hope and her voice softened. "Then prove it. Spend the rest of the day with me. We can swim or rent a movie or go down to the barn and spend some time with the horses. I'll fix dinner and—"

"No." He looked over at her and then quickly away. "I can't. I've got some paperwork to go over, and I've already made plans for dinner at the Cattleman's Club."

"I see," she said slowly. And she did. Despite everything she'd just said, he was making a deliberate choice to shut her out the same way he had in the past. She gathered Rosie a little closer, suddenly in need of comfort. "You're not even going to try, are you?"

"Try what?"

"To give our relationship a chance."

His whole body tensed. "Dammit, I told you before, I just…can't."

"Oh, Sterling, even Clarry knows you better than that! I know you've been hurt, but if you could just reach down and find it in you to give us a chance…"

His face might have been carved from granite. "I've said I'm sorry. I'll try to watch my schedule. Other than that, I don't know what you expect me to do."

She considered his unyielding expression. It didn't take her long to see that it was no use—an opinion that was confirmed when he broke the ensuing silence with a faintly exasperated sigh.

"Are we done?"

"Yes." *In more ways than you know,* she thought sadly.

She didn't say a word this time when he reached for his cell phone.

Sterling's head snapped up as the door to his den flew open.

"Well, I hope you're proud of yourself!" Maxine marched into the room, planted her hands on her hips and glared at him.

Very carefully, he set down the prospectus he'd spent the past hour trying to study. It just wasn't his day, he thought blackly. First there'd been that painful conversation with Susan. God knows, he'd done his best to stay out of her way so as not to do anything more to hurt her, but had she appreciated his effort? Hell, no.

Now this. He stared impatiently at his housekeeper. "You want to explain what you're talking about?"

"I'm talking about your wife. Don't think I don't notice what goes on around here. I've seen the way you've given the girl the cold shoulder all week and I know she's moved back into her own bedroom. But this!" She threw up her hands. "I don't know what you did on that trip to Moran's, but whatever it is you ought to be ashamed of yourself!"

His lips compressed. "Your opinion is duly noted. Now I'd appreciate it if you'd leave me alone." He reopened the prospectus. "Be sure to close the door on your way out."

"Oh, no, *Mr.* Churchill." Maxine advanced on his desk like an avenging angel. "You may be able to bully that sweet thing you married," she exclaimed, "but not me. Not when she's upstairs right now, her poor little face as white as a sheet, packing her things—"

"What?" His head shot up. "What are you talking about, Maxine?"

"I told you. She's leaving. She told me she'd miss the Oasis, and me, but under the circumstances she couldn't possibly stay here—"

Sterling was on his feet, across the room and out the door before she had a chance to finish the sentence. Striding down the hall, he told himself the housekeeper had to be mistaken. Susan wouldn't leave. She couldn't. She was his wife. They had an agreement.

Even so, he took the stairs two at a time.

He marched double time down the upper hall, only to come to an abrupt stop when her bedroom door suddenly opened.

Out stepped Susan, a suitcase in one hand and Rosie's leash in the other. She stopped dead at the sight of him, the puppy on her heels.

"What do you think you're doing?" he demanded.

She took a deep breath. "I'm taking the dog and I'm going."

"Going where?"

"Back to my house in Royal."

He struggled to hold onto his temper. "Don't be ridiculous, Susan. You can't do that."

A little bit of color came into her pale cheeks. "Yes, I can. I called my landlord. My place is still available and he said he'd be happy to have me back. I'll send someone out for the rest of my stuff in a few days, after I'm settled."

Damned if she didn't sound serious. He felt a faint stirring of something he told himself firmly wasn't fear. "You're not being reasonable."

"Actually, you're wrong," she said quietly. "This is the first reasonable thing I've done all week."

"And just what does that mean?"

"It means a lot of things. But the only one that matters is that I can't stay here anymore. Not now. Not like this. I want more for our child." She lifted her chin a notch. "I want more for myself."

"Well, I sure as Sam Hill can provide for both of you a hell of a lot better than you can by yourself—"

"Oh, Sterling, this isn't about money, and you know it."

"Then you explain it to me, Susan. Because I thought we had a deal."

She gave him a searching look, then slowly nodded. "All right. I'll try."

She was silent a moment, as if trying to decide how

to begin. Even so, he certainly didn't expect her to start where she did.

She took a deep breath, then slowly released it. "I thought a very long time before I decided to have a child. And one of the first things I realized was that if I wanted to be a good parent, I was going to have to change. I was going to have to stop being so afraid."

She set down her suitcase, her brown eyes becoming distant and thoughtful. "Ever since my parents died, I've sort of been living in the shadows, using shyness as an excuse to keep a low profile. I guess I thought that would keep me safe, make me a smaller target for what I'd learned could be a cruel and capricious Fate.

"And it did. Except that I was so very, very lonely. And though there weren't any more sorrows, there weren't any joys, either. Until finally I realized that the only way I was ever going to have anything worth keeping was if I took some chances." She suddenly lost her distant look and focused in on him. "That's what getting pregnant was, Sterling. It was taking a chance on life.

"So was marrying you, in a way. I honestly thought I could do it. I thought that as long as I had the baby, it would be enough for you and I just to be friends. But then—" for an instant her face lit up "—I fell in love with you. And I can't change it. Any more than I can pretend not to feel what I do."

She glanced down at the floor and fell silent. When she looked up, her eyes were filled with pain. "Earlier today, out in the truck, however, I finally realized that I can't expect you to pretend, either. And that's why I'm leaving."

He took a firm grip on himself. No matter how affected he might be by what she'd just said, this was not the time to lose sight of the bottom line—and that was her staying. "What's that supposed to mean?"

"Just that I've thought about everything you said. And if it's really true you can't love anyone, that includes the baby. Which means that anything you did for our child would be done out of duty—the way it was for you with your mother." She shook her head. "We both know how that turned out. I love you, Sterling, but I won't let you do that to our baby. I won't let you do it to me. We both deserve better."

He stared at her, stunned to the depths of his soul that she would ever dream of comparing him to his mother.

She picked up her suitcase and moved past him down the hall. Stooping to pick up Rosie as she reached the stairs, she paused, almost as if she expected him to say something. When he didn't, she said softly, "Goodbye, Sterling." With that, she was gone.

It was just like Teresa all over again.

He felt a stab of pain like a knife through his heart. It jerked him out of his temporary paralysis, and for one mad moment he was tempted to go after her.

Abruptly he came to his senses. With a heartfelt oath, he spun around and strode toward his bedroom, telling himself firmly that he didn't give a damn what she did. After all, this was pretty much what he'd expected the second he'd realized things were getting out of hand. Why not? His mother, Teresa—they'd both walked away, one emotionally, one literally, simply because they didn't care enough to stay.

That's right. At least with Susan she's leaving because she loves you too much...

The thought stopped him dead in his tracks.

But only for a second. He shook it off and resumed his march, telling himself not to be stupid. After all,

CAROLINE CROSS173

there was no way she could love him and still believe
he was like his mother, he thought, striding into his bedroom and slamming the door.

His jaw bunched. No matter what she thought, it
wasn't true. There was no way he would ever treat a
child of his with the sort of distant reserve that was all
he'd ever known from his mother. He wanted this baby.
And he was going to be a damn good father. And for
Susan to even *suggest* that he'd ever do anything that
might wound their child was inexcusable. Hadn't he
vowed that his son or daughter would have a better,
happier childhood than he had?

Damn straight he had.

*So? Didn't you also vow to love, honor and cherish
Susan?*

It wasn't the same thing, he thought angrily. With
Susan, all he'd ever intended was to have a marriage of
convenience. And he would never have done that if he'd
thought for a moment she'd get some foolish notion in
her head that she was in love with him. Much less that
he'd ever be unwise enough to love her back—

The imprudent thought froze him in place. Instantly
he tried to deny it, telling himself he was mistaken. But
once unleashed, the bone deep truth of it refused to go
away. Like a house of cards in a wind storm, the denial
he'd been using to keep himself safe blew apart.

He sank down onto the bed, not quite able to take it
in.

He loved her.

All right. So what if he did? It didn't change anything,
he told himself a little desperately. So what if he suddenly understood the terror he'd felt that day at the doctor's at the thought of anything happening to her. So
what if the urgency he'd felt that night now made sense.

Did it really matter that he must have known even then that he loved her? Or that he'd tried to express it in the only way he could?

Yeah, it does, you bastard. Because it also explains why you panicked when you found out she loved you, too. Go on. Admit it. You were afraid you'd never be able to survive if later she changed her mind.

He took a deep breath, shame splintering through him as he finally faced the truth: he'd hurt her to protect himself.

And now she was gone.

Oh, God. What had he done?

She was not going to cry. No matter what.

Eyes burning, throat tight, Susan walked doggedly down the Oasis's long driveway, mentally sending Royal's only cabdriver a bouquet of flat tires. Of all the times for him not to show up, why did it have to be today?

Not that anything else was going her way. The hot sun was beginning to give her a headache. The puppy was starting to lag. Her high-heeled sandals were not made for walking, her chest hurt from the effort of not crying and her heart—oh, her heart was definitely breaking.

Despite all that, Susan knew she'd made the right choice. After everything that had happened—and the one thing that hadn't—there was no way she could stay.

She swallowed, a little ashamed to admit how much she'd hoped the shock of her leaving would prompt Sterling into making a declaration of love.

How foolish. Clearly she'd let her feelings for him cloud her judgment and convince her of something that didn't exist. Yet even so, she didn't regret the things she'd said. She'd needed to say them almost as much as he'd needed to hear them.

Still, given his expression after she'd likened him to his mother, she was pretty sure she'd burned her bridges and then some. Now, she had no choice but to get on with her life.

Even if that meant walking the whole way to Royal.

Unfortunately, the trip might take a while. With a tired sigh, she juggled the end of the leash as she switched the heavy, unwieldy suitcase to her other hand. Until she'd set off on this walk, she hadn't realized how spoiled she'd become the past month. It was going to take a while to get reaccustomed to not having a car to drive. Just as it would feel strange not to have Maxine around to fuss over her. And she would definitely miss the Oasis's expanses of green, and even the horses...

Of course, none of that compared to what it was going to be like not to see Sterling over the breakfast table in the morning. Or hear him outside in the early evening, whistling for Cassie. Or feel his warm, solid weight beside her in the bed at night...

Her mouth trembled. Swallowing a painful lump in her throat, she tried to walk a little faster, only to stop instead when the leash went taut behind her. Rosie, it seemed, had had enough of this adventure. "Come on, sweetie," she coaxed, wearily turning around.

Her breath caught. Eight feet away at the end of the leash stood Sterling, holding the puppy in his hands.

For a second she thought she might faint. "Oh, my. How—how did you get here?"

"I walked," he said grimly, his gray eyes locked on her face. "You were so lost in thought, I guess you didn't hear me." He set down the dog. Closing the distance between them, he took the leash and the suitcase out of her trembling hands and set them down as well.

"But what—" she had to take a calming breath before she could go on "—are you doing here?"

He straightened, suddenly so close she could feel the heat radiating off his big body. "I'm not letting you go, Susan."

"Oh, please." Her anguish was very real. Walking away once was all she could handle; she didn't think she had the strength to do it again. "Please, don't. This is hard enough as it is—"

"I know." Before she could divine his intent, he reached out and caught one of her hands in his own. "I know, and it's all my fault. I've been nine kinds of fool and I promise, if you'll just forgive me, I'll spend the rest of my life making it up to you."

Her heart seemed to stand still. "You will?"

He nodded, looking somberly down at her. "Back at the house, you said you'd come to realize you weren't ever going to have anything worthwhile if you didn't take some chances. Well, I'm here to take one now— the biggest one of my life. I love you, Susan. I love you, and the baby, and I don't think I can stand it if you leave me."

It was a declaration of love and then some. She looked up into his dear, dear face, seeing the love and the fear, the hope and the need he could no longer hide—and burst into tears.

"Aw, dammit." Panic mixed with desperation in his voice. "Susan, sweetheart, don't cry. Please. I'm sorry. I'm so damn sorry for everything. I swear if you'll have me, I'll do better…"

She threw herself into his arms.

Sterling squeezed his eyes shut, saying a silent prayer

of thankfulness as he wrapped his arms around her and felt her small, precious body against his. Relief rocketed through him and for a second his knees felt mortifyingly weak. He pulled her even closer and buried his head in her hair, stroking her slender back and doing his best to show her how sorry he was.

Finally she quieted. He reluctantly loosened his hold as she took a step back and looked up at him. Her lipstick was gone, her eyes were red and her cheeks flushed—and he'd never seen anyone half so beautiful. "Are you okay?"

"Yes."

"Does this—" he cleared his throat, his voice rough with emotion "—does this mean you'll give me a second chance?"

"Yes." She reached up and cupped his face in her hands. "Oh, yes. I love you, Sterling. So much. And nothing will ever change that."

A sheen of moisture glazed his eyes. "I love you, too, sweetheart."

Dipping his head, he kissed her, hot, sweet and tender. And this time, he held nothing back.

Epilogue

It was a perfect Texas night. The air was mild, the breeze a mere whisper. Stars twinkled in the vast indigo sky, while a huge yellow moon cast a gentle light.

The Oasis glittered like a debutante all gussied up for her coming-out. Thousands of little white lights twinkled in the trees and bushes and along the fences. Huge pots of fragrant flowers lined the patio steps, and dozens of candles bobbed on the swimming pool and flickered atop a forest of matching umbrella tables. A local band played a soulful love song, while white-coated waiters circulated among the near-hundred guests.

Sterling gazed down on the lively scene from the master bedroom window. He pulled Susan, who was nestled in his arms with her back to his front, a little closer, gratified as she gave a happy sigh.

"I think our party's a success," she said softly.

He rubbed his cheek against her hair. "I think you're

right." Their belated wedding reception had been in full swing for the past two hours.

"It's sure nice to see Callie and Hank again."

He watched as the couple in question swayed slowly across the dance floor, Callie's blond head nestled next to Hank's dark one. "Yeah, it is."

"They look so happy."

"They should. Theirs had to be the world's longest honeymoon."

"Actually, according to Callie it's still going on," Susan said softly.

He tightened his arms around her. "They aren't the only ones."

She smiled, and for a few minutes they were quiet, simply enjoying their stolen time together.

Susan broke the silence. "Who's that?" She nodded toward a tall, dark-haired man who stood alone, a pensive expression on his face as he watched the dancing.

"That's Greg Hunt."

"The state's top attorney?"

He nodded, brushing his cheek against her hair. "Uh-huh."

"He doesn't look very happy."

An expression of tenderness chased across Sterling's face at the concern he could hear in her voice. He, too, thought Greg looked slightly forlorn, and he couldn't help but wonder if it had something to do with Princess Anna. But he wasn't about to say so since he didn't want to worry his tender-hearted little wife. "I'm sure he's fine."

"Maybe," she said thoughtfully. "Oh, look—there's Becky. Doesn't she look nice?"

Following her gaze, he saw his friend walk into view down below. She was dressed in a slim, indigo sheath that was wonderful with her bright red hair. "Yeah, she does."

"I don't think we're the only ones who think so, either."

Susan watched as Forrest Cunningham, who was standing by the fence, suddenly stiffened when he caught sight of the slender rancher.

Behind her she felt Sterling shrug. "I didn't get you up here to talk about Forrest and Becky," he informed her, loosening his hold and turning her around to face him.

Her lips curved. "You didn't?"

"Nope." He shook his head.

"Then why did you bring me here?"

He glanced pointedly at the bed.

"Sterling!" She gave a soft little laugh and shook *her* head. "I'm afraid you're going to have to wait."

He sighed, but there was amusement dancing in his smoky eyes. "I thought you might say that."

They smiled at each other. "I guess if I can't entice you into bed, I might as well go ahead and give you this." He pulled a flat, royal-blue velvet jeweler's box from his pocket and placed it in her hands.

"Oh, my..." The box felt warm from the contact with his body. She glanced from it to him questioningly.

"Go on. Open it."

Carefully she did, her breath catching as she saw what lay inside. Nestled against a bed of blue satin was a single, heart-shaped diamond on a gleaming gold chain. "Oh, Sterling, it's beautiful," she exclaimed.

"It's for our one-month anniversary." He picked it up and fastened it around her neck. He hesitated, then added quietly, "And so you'll never forget that my heart is yours to keep."

Tenderness washed through her. She slid her hand around his neck and tugged his head down to hers. "Thank you," she whispered, her soft lips brushing his mouth.

His arms came around her and for a long, satisfying moment there was nobody in the world but the two of them.

Finally Sterling lifted his head, resting his forehead against hers. "You're sure I can't talk you into bed?" he asked huskily.

Susan smiled, knowing he was teasing and loving him for it. "Later," she promised.

"Yeah, I guess you're right. Because once I do get you there, I don't intend to get out for a while."

"That sounds perfect to me."

Hand in hand, they walked out of the room and went to celebrate their marriage.

* * * * *

Don't miss the next installment of the
Texas Cattleman's Club—
*when Forrest Cunningham attempts to make
good on his marriage pact to Becky Sullivan in*

BILLIONAIRE BRIDEGROOM

*by Peggy Moreland
Coming to you from Silhouette Desire
in October 1999.
And now for a sneak preview of*
BILLIONAIRE BRIDEGROOM,
please turn the page.

Royal, Texas, 1987

Sweat poured down Forrest Cunningham's face. After chasing steers through the scrub brush all afternoon under a hot West Texas sun, his boots—and his butt—were dragging as he led his horse to the rails of the corral.

With his thoughts focused on the beer iced down and waiting for him in a cooler propped on the tailgate, he tied his horse to the corral's top rail, then cut a quick path to the rear of the truck. He fished a cold brew from the cooler, popped the top, then, with a sigh of pure pleasure, lifted the beer.

"Hey, Woody! Wait! I get first sip!"

He sighed and dutifully lowered the can. It was a ritual. Becky always got the first sip. And Forrest allowed it. Just as he allowed her to call him "Woody" and live to tell it. Five years his junior, and a neighbor for as long as he could remember, Becky Sullivan was like a kid sister to him, and, as such, enjoyed full rights.

He angled his head, a grin tugging at the corner of his mouth, as he watched her charging toward him, her long legs churning, her hand flattened on the top of her battered cowboy hat to keep the wind from ripping it off her head.

She skidded to a stop in front of him and snatched the can from his hand. She bumped up the brim of her hat, knocking it off, and thick red hair fell to pool around her shoulders. Lifting the beer in a silent toast, she shot Forrest a wink, then tipped back her head and drank deeply.

Forrest knew damn good and well he could kiss that beer goodbye. Becky Sullivan might be only eighteen, but she drank like a man.

Truth be told, Becky could do most things as well as a man. She could out-ride, out-rope and out-shoot just about any male in Ward county. He supposed she'd learned these skills out of necessity, being as she'd pretty much raised herself and was responsible for whatever work was accomplished on her family's ranch, the Rusty Corral.

He fished out a new can from the cooler. After popping the top, be hooked an arm around her slim shoulders and headed her toward the shade provided by the trailer and plopped down.

Shoulder to shoulder they stared out across the pasture, sipping their beers, while the cattle bawled pitifully in the corral, the silence between them a comfortable one.

"The Texas Cattleman's Ball is coming up in a couple of weeks," Becky offered after a bit.

Forrest pulled the brim of his hat over his eyes and settled in for a nap. "Yeah, it is."

"Who're you takin'?"

"Lyndean Sawyer from over in Midland."

"Haven't heard you mention her name before."

Something in her voice made him nudge his hat from his eyes to peer at her. She was squinting hard at the sun, the corners of her mouth pulled down into a frown. "No. Just a date," he said slowly. When her frown deepened, he asked, "Why do you ask?"

She lifted her beer, her movements tense and jerky, and took a sip. "Just curious."

"Are you going to the ball this year?"

"Nope. Nobody asked me."

Surprised by the splotch of red that suddenly appeared on her cheeks, he gave her a poke with his beer can. "Oh, come on. A pretty girl like you? Boys'll be tripping all over themselves for the chance to ask you to the ball. Just you wait and see."

As he stared at her, he was sure that he saw her chin quiver. And were those tears making her eyes sparkle? Naw, he told himself. Becky wasn't the crying type. Yet, as he watched, a fat tear slipped over her lid and down her cheek.

He tossed aside his beer and slung an arm around her shoulder, drawing her against his side. "Aw, Becky. Don't cry."

She lifted her head and turned to look at him. "Woody, do you think I'll ever get married?"

The hopelessness in her voice touched his heart and made him a little uneasy. The word *marriage* always had that effect on Forrest. "I don't know, Becky. I suppose you will, if you want to."

"I don't think I will," she murmured after a long

moment. "All the guys just think of me as one of them, never as a female." She choked back a laugh that sounded dangerously close to a sob. "I can see it now. Thirty-years-old, a dried up old maid and still working the Rusty Corral all by myself."

Forrest heard the defeat in her voice, as well as the loneliness. "Tell you what, Becky," he offered. "If you're not married by your thirtieth birthday, hell, I'll marry you."

She turned to look at him, her eyes wide. "Do you mean it?"

"Damn straight." He pecked a kiss on her cheek, then scooted back against the trailer, dipping the brim of his hat low over his eyes again. "Of course, by the time you turn thirty, you'll probably be married and have a litter of snot-nosed kids hanging on to your belt loops."

Or at least he hoped she did. Forrest Cunningham was a man whose word was as good as law...but he sure as hell wasn't planning on getting married.

If you enjoyed what you just read,
then we've got an offer you can't resist!

Take 2 bestselling love stories FREE!

Plus get a FREE surprise gift!

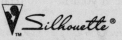

THE
FORTUNES
OF TEXAS

*Membership in this family has its privileges
...and its price.
But what a fortune can't buy,
a true-bred Texas love is sure to bring!*

Coming in October 1999...

The Baby Pursuit

by

LAURIE PAIGE

When the newest Fortune heir was kidnapped, the
prominent family turned to Devin Kincaid to find the
missing baby. The dedicated FBI agent never expected
his investigation might lead him to the altar with
society princess Vanessa Fortune....

THE FORTUNES OF TEXAS continues with
Expecting... In Texas by **Marie Ferrarella**,
available in November 1999 from
Silhouette Books.

Available at your favorite retail outlet.

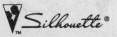

Silhouette®

SILHOUETTE®
Desire®

Get ready to enter the exclusive, masculine world of the...

TEXAS Cattleman's Club

Silhouette Desire®'s powerful new miniseries features five wealthy Texas bachelors—all members of the state's most prestigious club—who set out on a mission to rescue a princess...and find true love!

TEXAS MILLIONAIRE—August 1999
by Dixie Browning (SD #1232)
CINDERELLA'S TYCOON—September 1999
by Caroline Cross (SD #1238)
BILLIONAIRE BRIDEGROOM—October 1999
by Peggy Moreland (SD #1244)
SECRET AGENT DAD—November 1999
by Metsy Hingle (SD #1250)
LONE STAR PRINCE—December 1999
by Cindy Gerard (SD #1256)

Available at your favorite retail outlet.

Silhouette®